NEBRASKA

ALSO BY GEORGE WHITMORE

The Confessions of Danny Slocum

NEBRASKA

A NOVEL BY
George Whitmore

GROVE PRESS
New York

Published by Grove Press, Inc.
920 Broadway
New York, N.Y. 10010

This book was written with the assistance of the Edward Albee Foundation and the MacDowell Colony.

The author gratefully acknowledges permission to reprint lyrics from *Light My Fire* by The Doors. © 1967 Doors Music Company. All rights reserved. Used by permission.

Library of Congress Cataloging-in-Publication Data

Whitmore, George, 1945–
Nebraska.

I. Title.
PS3573.H527N44   1987   813'.54   87–12113
ISBN 0–802–10026–0

Designed by Irving Perkins Associates, Inc.
Manufactured in the United States of America
First Edition 1987

10 9 8 7 6 5 4 3 2 1

for Victor

1956

YOU would never listen to me and now look what's happened!" Mama fainted dead away. The next thing I knew, I woke up with my leg gone.

She meant I would refuse to walk when I could run. I would not look both ways before I crossed the street. I would forget and have to be sent back to the store when it was already dark.

I felt sorry for the man who hit me. When they put me in the ambulance, he was sitting there on the curb, an honest working man in coveralls.

I would run. I ran blind—I was twelve years old but more a baby. In my imagination, there were worse things along that stretch of road than getting hit.

"What is wrong with you?"

I was a case, that's for sure. My arm was broke. The skin was off whole parts of me. I had stitches I didn't even know about. When my sisters came to see me they both cried out.

I had two doctors. The first one said "That child keeps wetting the bed his stump will never heal." The other said "Sure you can take him home but how will you take care of him?"

Mama said "We will take good care of him. He is the only one we have."

I was in and out. I lost whole days. I heard Mama saying "We're going to be paying off the bills for the rest of our lives."

I tried to think how I could help. I heard her say "Now I guess we won't have to buy that bike." I cried because I could not have my paper route now.

3

When I was in the hospital, I was like the lady in the magician's box, who must smile and smile as the blades get slipped into her. When I came home, Mama tried to keep this torture up as they had told her to. However I begged, Mama would poke and prod. Mama would flip-flop me morning and night. Mama wore herself clean out with tormenting.

When I was in the hospital, I heard the nurses say about a little girl who died "Do you know what they said? They opened up that little tyke and found such a tumor there she must have been in terrible pain all her life. But you see she didn't never know it. She must of thought This is just life."

I lay there thinking To be in terrible pain and not know it because it was all you ever knew. And maybe this is true. Maybe you just don't know it. Maybe if you're lucky you get numb, for all I know is, after a while that chawed up lost leg was all I felt—even if it was buried somewhere in some city dump, that lost leg was more real than my real body. Answer when I'm talking! Mama yelled at me but I was deaf and dumb. At night I turned that lost leg over and over and over like a new limb held in my hands and after a while there wasn't anything they could do to me that hurt anymore.

Mama was wore out. She worked all day at Monkey Wards. She waited on tables on the top floor. I liked it there because you could sit on that balcony and watch all the shoppers far below crowding up against the counters.

I lived with Mama, Betty and Dolores in a half house—each step on the stairway there was supposedly the same as the one next door. We rented our half longer than anyone else.

When I came home from the hospital it was summer already. Mama had a real hospital bed waiting for me out on the sleeping porch—they could not get it up the stairs. She made Betty and Dolores wait on me. I thought Mama was so wonderful.

This sleeping porch was on the side of the house and lilac bushes screened it from the street. In early summer those blossoms hung off every branch like big bunches of grapes but through the chinks in the bushes I could see people passing by.

Most days the only sign of life all day was a sprinkler on the lawn across the street but every day at four the paperboy who got my route would come whooshing by, pumping hard.

I watched TV and did my puzzle books—I was a puzzle freak and went through dozens of those books each week. I even had made up puzzles myself. This was my only talent and had once got me in the paper.

They came out and took my picture. They printed it in the paper over the caption

Boy Puzzle Whiz

But now the neighbors did not go by our house and say as I hoped they would "That's the house where the puzzle whiz lives." They said "Look at that yard, it's disgraceful, it's all dirt."

When I got my cast off, they told Mama I was not yet to go to physical therapy in spite of all they had promised. Sometimes my pee was still pink. I lived in fear.

"Get ready to die," Dolores said setting down my lunch.

One day in the middle of that summer, Mama came to me with something in her hand. She sat down on the edge of the bed.

"I found this in the hamper when I was sorting the wash," Mama said, letting my handkerchief uncrumple. "I know boys have urges," she said, "that are mostly natural."

I thought of lying and saying I just blew my nose in it.

She held the handkerchief up. "I don't want to see this ever again, understand?"

I did. I nodded. But a door closed in me. Mama had shut it.

I was, you see, the only male in that household until Uncle Wayne came home.

For all my childhood it seemed Uncle Wayne was a sailor. He was away in the navy so long I didn't know what he looked like anymore.

We all worshipped Uncle Wayne the way you worship movie stars. A postcard from Uncle Wayne was a holy relic. We all awaited news from him.

When I had my accident, a package arrived for me from Honolulu. In it was a plastic ukulele. You could strum on the strings or play it with a crank. It played Lovely Hula Hands.

So all my childhood Uncle Wayne was sailing around the world from one dangerous port to another. I found out later of course he had not been so close to combat, only dispatched some fighters into the war zone, but when Uncle Wayne came home he might as well have been the greatest hero.

When Uncle Wayne came home he came up to my bed and stood there grinning and said "What the hell happened to you, Skeezix?"

T HE first thing you noticed was the ring on his little finger. It was a diamond engagement ring. Betty perched on the arm of his chair and picked up his hand.

"What's this, Uncle Wayne?"

"This here, Betty, was recently returned to me by a young lady in San Diego."

"Oh Uncle Wayne, you mean you was engaged?"

"For a brief while there I was, kiddo."

But when he came downstairs later it was gone.

Women made a terrible fuss over him. Aunt Eileen almost

peed her pants to see her baby brother when he walked in the door. He tossed down his white duffle bag and the girls were jumping up and down but Mama stayed in the kitchen frying chicken and he had to go in after her. She was crying too.

That night we had a picnic in our back yard. Wayne carried me out and laid me on the air mattress to Dad's old sleeping bag. We ate chicken and potato salad and watermelon. By the time we finished eating it was dark. But we stayed out there talking and laughing at Uncle Wayne's jokes—I thought he was so funny. There was just the sink light on in the house and a blue glow from the TV next door where you could hear the sound of laughter from New York.

It was so hot. Everyone agreed it was a real Nebraska summer to welcome Wayne home.

Everyone was amazed how fast the plane had brought him home.

"I bet you ain't even lost your sea-legs," Uncle Sparky said. "Those ships are just like floating cities, ain't they?" he said.

"Sure are," said Uncle Wayne.

"What was your ship called, Uncle Wayne?"

"My ship was the Alameda."

"Will you miss the Alameda, Uncle Wayne?"

"Why, hell's bells, honey. The Alameda was my whole life."

But now he announced he was going away again soon to open up his new garage in California. He was going to be a partner with his shipboard pal the Chief. We all yelled No, but he held his hands up and said California is the place.

Then at that very moment the phone rang long distance. Uncle Wayne bounded up the stairs.

It was so hot the birds hung like they were dead in the trees. We were all silent. We didn't have anything to say to each other. We could hear Uncle Wayne on the phone.

"No, I'm sorry, Miss," he said, "Mr. Wayne Smith is not here."

Then he came out back and said that was all arranged ahead

of time so the Chief could call person to person and know he was home safe but not have to pay for the call.

By the time Eileen stood up and dusted off her skirt telling Sparky they must go home, so many empty beer bottles lined those back steps it looked like you could walk up into the house on them.

Mama went inside and washed up the pots and pans Betty and Dolores had conveniently forgot. Dolores went up to set her hair. Betty sat there next to Uncle Wayne on the blanket with her head on his shoulder like he was her drive-in dream date.

"Why can't you stay in Nebraska forever, Uncle Wayne?"

"Well soon you can visit me, can't you? Wouldn't you like to take a bus all the way across the U.S.?"

"Only if it was to see you."

"She gets car sick," I said.

Uncle Wayne stroked her cheek.

The porch light came on and Mama, moths around her head, said it was time for bed. So Uncle Wayne picked me up in his arms and carried me inside.

Uncle Wayne smelled of sweat and whiskey and beers and Camels—Grandma once said How bad Grandpa's long-johns stink from his chewing tobacco when I put them through the mangle!

Before I went to sleep, Mama gave me a sponge bath and bandaged the stump as you must do.

"Will Uncle Wayne live in his own house in California?" I asked her.

"Where else would he live?"

"Will he own a convertible?"

"He'd like to I bet."

"Will he have a swimming pool?"

We learned about the Chief. First of all he was Uncle Wayne's best friend and also his chief petty officer. Second, the nickname Uncle Wayne gave him on the Alameda, the Shadow, was given him for being a great practical joker. The Chief came from Chula Vista, a town near Mexico, and had a legendary capacity for booze. According to Uncle Wayne, the Chief was going to borrow money from his brother-in-law to open up that garage.

Uncle Wayne spoke of his plans at the breakfast table. Mama was upset for he was her nearest and dearest and had been away so long. "This is so fast," she said. "Why can't you boys open up a garage here in Lincoln?"

"Because the Chief's out on the Coast, Sis."

"But why can't he come here?"

"Because all his connections is out there, you see."

Mama shook her head. "You go out there and I'm afraid you will never come back home."

"Sure I will."

"And what about our Dad?"

She did not mention Grandma. Uncle Wayne had really come home to Mama because she was the only one who was once a real mother to him.

G RANDPA worked on the railroad so all their married life, Grandpa and Grandma were never out of earshot of it. Grandma said when Mama was little they lived in a house so close to the tracks she kept the front door locked and hid the key—she was afraid one of the kids would fall off the porch in front of the train.

They lived in Warren some thirty miles from us. Their house there was for once only on a spur of the railroad so freight cars came by only once or twice a day, but at night the lights of every

9

auto going over the grade would shine in the downstairs window. I liked going to Grandpa and Grandma's because they had a gravel pit out back where you could play War and a big cellar full of busted-up furniture and old magazines.

In truth there was not much good about this house where Grandpa and Grandma had finally settled and I myself lived so much of my life. Being a man who worked with his hands, you would have thought Grandpa would be handy around his own house, but he never fixed a thing on it and everything was always falling apart.

This house which stood next to a stinking bayou started out as a mere shack and just grew one little room at a time. The only good thing about it I thought was a bathroom Dad built onto it off the kitchen before I was even born—it had beautiful fixtures and stood on a slab of concrete, so the year the river came up over the town dykes and the bayou flooded, Grandpa's house floated away but Dad's bathroom stayed put. A big truck hauled the house back to the foundations.

We used to go to Grandpa's for dinner every other Sunday at twelve on the dot. We all sat around the table in the kitchen and watched Grandpa stuff himself.

He took giant helpings. He could eat four or five big slices of meat loaf in a sitting. He would take a big mess of mashed potatoes and make a volcano filled with gravy. He liked to mix everything up—beans, meat and potatoes would all go into Grandpa's mouth together.

Grandpa had a handsome Studebaker but he liked it too much to drive it. So when Uncle Wayne arrived in Lincoln Grandpa said Let Mohammed come to the Mountain. But Uncle Wayne didn't go. He hated his old family home. After lots of phone calls Grandpa and Grandma came to Lincoln after all only because Sparky went and drove them.

And after all when they met after such a long time, Grandpa kissed Uncle Wayne on the ear and held him like he would like to dance with him—Grandpa dance! Grandpa was so big around it would take two girls to hold him in their arms.

All of us were scared of Grandpa but not Uncle Wayne. All of us knew the story of how Uncle Wayne would never let Grandpa whip him—not since Grandpa cornered him in the cellar one time and Wayne tried to slice him with a knife.

I myself had a first memory of Grandpa. It was him bouncing me on his knee and making me so sick because I was only two and afraid he would not stop—he might bounce me until my eyes popped out of my head and I bit off my poor tongue.

When Uncle Wayne told Grandpa his plans about California, Grandpa was mystified. He had just figured all that time Wayne would work on the railroad when he got out.

"But I told Ed the other day."

"Dad, I never said a thing about working on no damned railroad."

"I told him you'd call."

"I'm just here for a brief visit's all."

"You'll never get the benefits they got!"

This meant a great deal to Grandpa. Grandma was going to have a pension equal to one-third his current wage.

Uncle Wayne just laughed, covering his bad teeth—he forgot the navy fixed them for him free.

"Why the hell did you get yourself discharged then?" roared Grandpa. He was shaking. This was their life-long battle and Grandpa sensed he was losing again. He looked around for someone to yell at and decided to pick on Mama for the spoons—Grandma always had to keep spoons on the table for him in a cut-glass jar but Mama didn't.

"Why the hell can't you keep a proper house, Janet!"

"I am not going to work on no goddamned railroad."

"Well why the hell then did you get out of the navy?"

Grandma was twitching with nerves by now. Her fingers ran like spiders over the buttons on her dress.

11

"Wayne will make up his own mind," Mama was so bold as to say.

Then a tear formed in the corner of one of Grandpa's old yellow eyes—he figured maybe he could weep his way out of this. He said "This'll about kill your poor mother."

Grandma sat up in her chair.

Grandpa turned to Grandma and said "Now won't it!"

Grandma just about jumped out of her chair.

Wayne lit a Camel.

"I would like it," Grandma kind of squeaked, "if Wayne could move closer."

"Course you would!"

Uncle Wayne shrugged Grandpa off as if to say China was not far enough away from Nebraska to suit him but California would do.

That next week when he got a letter from the Chief he sat there in the living room on the sofa and snickered away at it.

"This man is such a card."

"Does he say anything about the loan from his brother-in-law, Uncle Wayne?"

Uncle Wayne flipped over the paper and kept on reading.

"I bet you miss the Chief, Uncle Wayne."

"I was with the man almost twenty-four hours a day, Skee-zix, three whole years you know."

"I wish the Shadow would come here."

"Well, Betty, you will get to meet him, won't you, when you come to California."

WHEN I was in the hospital my class made me a big
get-well card out of construction paper and everyone signed it,
but after I came home nobody visited but Wesley.

Wesley said all the kids were now taking the Red Cross water
safety class learning how to swim. He showed me the crawl
moving his arms like a windmill and kicking one leg into thin
air.

That summer Wesley got to go Summer Baptist Bible too—
Wesley had about the best life of any boy in Lincoln, Nebraska.
He was an only child. He lived in a big house with trees in front
and a two-car garage. He had a room full of toys like an ant
farm, a chemistry set and a Prince Valiant castle with rubber
men.

When Wesley came over to see me when I was laid up he
would bring his used comic books—Superman, Terry and the
Pirates, and horror comics where people got chopped up or
melted or burned or slashed to ribbons. Wesley and me would
argue over things like How much of you would blow up if a
hand-grenade went off when you were holding it? I said all of
you while Wesley said just the middle.

That summer Wesley and his family took a trip to the Bad-
lands in their Buick. The marvel of this car was that it had
air-conditioning, so Wesley's mama took her canary in a teeny
cage in the glove compartment and it didn't die.

Ever since I had to stop parochial school when Dad left,
Wesley was my best friend in public school. Before my accident
we spent Saturdays playing in the park or in the schoolyard, in

his room or at my house. We would sleep over and play games like Hearts or Clue.

Grownups liked Wesley because only kids got to see deep down he was mean as cat dirt. For instance, Wesley talked me into flushing Dolores' bobby-sox down the toilet once and once when we were walking down my alley to the drugstore he picked up rocks and broke every window in every garage along the way.

Wesley's own parents of course thought the sun rose and set with him. To them he could do no wrong so when his dad umpired our baseball games he never called Wesley out. And if Wesley got into a fight it was always the other kid's fault. If Wesley got bad grades or was punished for pinching girls the teacher didn't happen to like him.

One day Wesley and I spent the whole day going around with his wagon and picking up bottles out of trash cans to turn in for the deposit but when we got to the store Wesley said he deserved two-thirds because it was his wagon.

Yet this same Wesley was the only one who came to see me after my accident. I had known plenty of boys and girls who were sitting there in class one day then were gone and totally forgot the next. I figured I was now one of those.

I had only been a popular child once, for two days, when I got my picture in the paper as the Boy Puzzle Whiz, and I'm afraid I wasn't popular during my teenage years after I recovered from my accident either. I had few dates or friends, but I'm getting ahead of my story.

Pretty soon that summer Wesley was talking about the Scouts most of the time. He belonged to the Cubs—his den made a big Indian drum out of an old oil can and innertubes. But in the fall Wesley was going to become a real Boy Scout. He already had his Tenderfoot knots down perfect.

"This is the best troop in the whole world," he informed me.

tell when Dad crossed the line because he would get real quiet.

Dad was a Catholic, true. But when they finally had to get married because of Dolores, Grandpa put up no objections. What was he to do?

I believe Dad was more or less drunk every day after Mama married him yet he held down a decent job with the County and was a good provider. He was a handsome Irishman with red hair. Everyone forgave Dad anything.

Dad loved us but he would try and hurt us. He would whip us if he found our toys on the floor. Dad sober taking us to Mass was scary—we knew after he had to sit there without being able to have a drink one of us would get a spanking before we even had a chance to change out of our good clothes.

When Dad was real drunk, he would come home and slobber all over us he loved us so much. He would call Mama "cupcake." When he was not drinking they would fight more than if he was. Dad would call Mama things like "You dried up old c——t!"

Mama tried to change Dad then she threw him out. Yet she always relented when he came crawling back.

Therefore when Dad jumped at the chance to work in St. Louis for more money than anyone had ever saw in his life no one said Oh don't leave us. When Dad was gone no one said I wish Dad was here, or Gee I miss Dad, because we didn't.

Dad worked building a bridge in St. Louis then went back to Missouri to built another bridge. He sent us lots of money. We lived in a nice house. We had a car. I had a dog named Rickey.

Then Dad showed up one afternoon and told Mama he wanted his freedom. Then he went back to St. Louis.

When us kids got home from school, Mama was locked in the bathroom. We got so scared we went next door to the neighbors and the man broke down our bathroom door.

For a week Mama stayed in bed with the blinds drawn and Grandma took care of us.

Then one night Mama got out of bed and made us hotdogs. We still didn't know what happened. All Grandma would say is that Dad and Mama had another one of their fights. That night Mama gave us ice cream for dessert and sat down to watch us eat it. Then she said "Your Dad is living in St. Louis for good."

Betty started bawling and I did too. Mama didn't say Stop, it will be all right. She got up and went back into her bedroom.

Dad did not keep in touch as he promised. He did not send money. He vanished. We had to move. I had to quit parochial school and start all over again. I had to give Rickey away because Mama said it cost an arm and a leg to feed him. We didn't ever have a car again.

"I hope he's dead," Betty said.

"I hope you die too," I said for I didn't give up loving Dad at that point.

Grandma and Grandpa McMullen lived in Arkansas. Only our Uncle Bill lived in Nebraska but if he knew at that time where Dad was he chose not to tell us. For a while Grandpa McMullen tried to help us out but Mama said they had plenty of worries of their own with their retarded daughter our aunt. Grandma McMullen said if Dad ever came to their home she would kick him out on his butt. He never did though. It was like Dad was dead.

Dad was not dead. He was in Denver. He had a new name. He didn't even bother to try and divorce Mama.

ALL that summer they called the hottest summer in human memory I lay on that porch still sick with sweat dripping off me. The County sent me back to the hospital to break my arm again. Parts of me were now yellow.

Uncle Wayne bided his time. Every week like clockwork for a while a letter came from the Chief but he still didn't, we guessed, have the money.

Uncle Wayne bought a second-hand Chevy for his drive to California. For a while there you could hear him out in the garage working on that old car. Next he took the Chevy to a body shop and had it painted Candy Apple Red.

Uncle Wayne involved himself in my rehabilitation. He gave me backrubs and saw to it I moved my limbs. He gave me a little rubber ball to squeeze because that developed your arm muscles. I squeezed that rubber ball until it popped apart along the seam.

Uncle Wayne also worked hard at keeping his own body in shape. He did sit-ups and push-ups. He had a pipe in the doorway for chin-ups. He was an inspiration to me.

Weekends Uncle Wayne would go out drinking with his friends Butchy, Martin and Harold. Harold and him would drive over to Warren to the Big Top or Butchy and Martin, because they lived in Warren, would come into Lincoln to the Blue Bird.

All these men were cutups together since they were boys, but for Uncle Wayne I saw it was not just like old times. He

19

complained to Mama "We grew apart, they ain't never been nowhere and never will."

"I ain't been nowhere either," Mama replied.

Mama didn't understand but I did. Since I could no longer be a sailor maybe I would be a merchant marine.

"With a peg leg?" Uncle Wayne said giving me a sponge bath. "Like Cap'n Hook?" he said. "I don't know why not."

I told Dolores I was going to sail around the world as Uncle Wayne had.

"The only place you're going to," she said, "is H-E-double-toothpicks."

"You're the one's going to hell," I said, "for all your mani-fold sins."

Dolores turned on me with her mouth hanging open. "What do you mean?"

"I saw you," I said from the fastness of my bed.

Dolores hit the ceiling. "Look here," she hissed at me, lean-ing across the sheets with hands clenched like claws—Mama was in the kitchen. "You ever tell anyone anything and I'll kill your guts."

Dolores was telling Mama she was going off babysitting or out to a movie or for a spin in a car with her girlfriends but those were just lies. She was sneaking off to meet someone and I found out who.

No wonder Mama wondered why Dolores was even lazier than usual. No wonder if Dolores was doing all this babysitting, she never had spending money.

Two nights that I knew of Dolores went up to bed and you heard her go to the bathroom and brush her teeth. Then you heard the springs cry out when she fell onto the bed. But after Mama turned out the lights and went to bed herself, down came Dolores carrying her shoes in one hand.

From my bed out on the sleeping porch with one eye squinted shut, I watched Dolores cross the living room and sneak into the kitchen—she didn't dare go out the front way because Mama's bedroom was over the door.

The second time I saw Dolores sneak out I turned over on my belly and watched through the lilacs as she tip-toed down the driveway to the sidewalk and down the street to the corner, then she gave a little Eek when someone said Boo and stepped out of the bushes. It was Uncle Wayne's old pal Harold and here Dolores was only sixteen.

I was doing some of my own sneaking though Mama soon put a stop to that. I found I could hold up my body on the edge of the bed and put my foot onto the floor. From there I could hop around my bed. Only my fear of falling hindered me from doing this often but soon I found I could move through the French doors and along the couch in the living room. I did this—just to move.

But one night Mama came down and caught me. I must have seemed a white ghost in the night for no one expected me anywhere but in that bed now and Mama screamed "What are you doing!" She rushed to me. "You want to end up back in that hospital again? You want to cost us one-hundred thousand dollars?"

I hopped and wobbled until Mama put my arms around her neck and dragged me to the bed.

"Why did you ever do such a crazy thing?" she moaned, at the end of her rope I think.

On the first of the month Uncle Wayne called the Chief long distance. He took the phone over to the stairs and spoke low into it.

"Well I was wondering," he said.

"That's just what I was thinking," he said.

"I can see that," he said.

"I guess we'll just have to," he said.

"Me too," he said.

"Do you?" he asked.

"This town is the asshole of creation," he said.

"You too," he said.

Then he hung up and went into the kitchen. When he came out with a beer in his hand I asked How is the Shadow?

Uncle Wayne looked at me like he had forgot I was alive. Then he looked at me almost with hatred.

"I mean the Chief," I said.

"Ain't you supposed to be asleep?"

"It's only nine."

"Little pitchers have big ears, don't they," he said and left the house. I heard a car door slam in the garage. Then I heard his radio playing

> Whenever we kiss
> I worry and wonder
> You're here in my arms
> But where is your heart?

and sadness stabbed me. I wanted to be sitting next to Uncle Wayne in his car listening to the radio but Uncle Wayne never even offered to carry me out to see that Chevy.

GRANDPA would not let up. Grandpa was like a leaky faucet in a rusty sink. If he could not talk Uncle Wayne into the railroad anymore, he thought now Uncle Wayne should aspire to work at Chicks with Sparky.

"But I have spoken to him at every opportunity," Sparky told Grandpa.

"You sure have, honey," said Aunt Eileen.

"I ran into him the other night when I just happened to stop off for a drink at the Blue Bird and we had quite a long talk," said Sparky.

"You done your best."

"Now this California feller," said Grandpa, "is like the pot at the end of the rainbow if you ask me."

"Chicks," said Sparky, "has been damned good to me."

Mama did what they asked. She brought up the subject. She was ironing his shirts. He was finishing supper.

Mama said "You know if things wasn't to work out in California—I mean they almost closed down Chicks two years ago, I don't know if I wrote you, but now it seems they're going great guns."

"Maybe next time they will wise up and close it down for good," Uncle Wayne said.

"What I mean to say."

"Fuck Chicks."

Mama hated profanity but she just grit her teeth and said "It doesn't strike me, Wayne, that things are going too well at the other end out there."

"They are going fine," Wayne said.

Then he slapped his palm hard on the table and said "Jesus! Why why why!" Uncle Wayne yelled. "Why can't anybody in the world let me live?"

Mama said "Well excuse me for living."

There was a silence then. I could hear the iron thump on the ironing board. Mama muttered You can live, but Uncle Wayne said No this is the way it always is, this is why I joined the navy lying about my age in the first place, and stormed out of the room.

He went upstairs. A few minutes later he stomped down the stairs and slammed the door. You could hear the garage door smack the fence post then that Chevy tore out of the driveway and laid rubber down the street.

23

Mama said Uncle Wayne almost killed Grandma and because she was so sick after she had him Mama had to take over.

Aunt Mona was gone. Uncle Walter was but a boy himself. Aunt Eileen was just like Dolores.

Mama was the one who got up in the night and changed Uncle Wayne. She gave him his bottle. She changed him and fed him breakfast before she went to school. When Mama came home for lunch she had to attend to Wayne. She took care of him in the night too. She was the one who gave him his dinner and put him to bed then she tried hard to do her homework. If he ever cried Mama was the one who must be there.

When Uncle Wayne was little he would not go to sleep without Mama—she had to be with him on the bed. Children would be playing outdoors. Mama would hear their cries in the twilight outside the window. They were playing Kick the Can and Blind Man's Bluff and It but Mama had to stay inside and very still on the bed because Uncle Wayne would lay on her arm so if she moved he would wake up and start crying again.

This is why Mama said in the hospital after my accident "You are not ever going to be robbed of your precious childhood."

"Course he won't," the doctor said smiling.

Late that night after their fight Uncle Wayne woke me up standing by my bed. He was pretty drunk.

"Didn't mean to wake you," he whispered, grinning from ear to ear down at me.

"That's all right," I said.

"Look at your sheet," he said like he just noticed though my bed was soaked with sweat every night. "Let's change that sheet," he said, switching on the lamp.

"That's all right," I said—he was teetering and I was afraid he would fall on me, but Uncle Wayne was already pulling the sheet out from under me and rolling me over to the other side. He knew how. He had changed my sheets lots of times because he loved me and wanted to take care of me. I was his only nephew.

He said in a whisper "Your mama didn't change your p.j.s either, did she, Skeezix?" He slid the sheet away. Quickly and efficiently as you would expect a serviceman to do Uncle Wayne changed the bed. He got me fresh p.j.s. He helped me off with the bottoms then when I was pulling the top off my head I felt Uncle Wayne's hand on my nuts.

"You're getting hair down there, Skeezix."

That's all. Then his hand was gone.

Inside my p.j. top I gulped. It smelled in there. I heard some old dog bark down the street.

When Uncle Wayne went upstairs, I lay back against the moonlight on my pillow. The new p.j.s felt good, almost cool. I felt my nuts. I felt the fuzz on them.

WESLEY went to junior high without me. The lilac leaves turned brown and curled up in front of my eyes. Uncle Wayne put up the storm windows on our side of the house.

Aunt Eileen was once a practical nurse so on the days the County came and Mama was at work she had an air of one who was sorely tried on my behalf. Concern lines creased her face. On one of these days we got a new doctor. He said "Is anyone helping this boy exercise?"

Aunt Eileen said she guessed so.

"Because it will soon be too late," he said. "What are these?"

The doctor held up some of my pills. Aunt Eileen said the regular County had prescribed these for me.

He threw them in the trash.

Aunt Eileen saw the doctor to the door then when she came back she fetched that little bottle out of the wastebasket and saw to it that I took my noon dose with orange juice.

Aunt Eileen would never go back into nursing, she said, for it would be like exchanging a crown for a mop, Sparky treated her so good.

She was his first and last but she herself was married three times before—Dad always said she had a screw loose for she married a whole string of men who beat her up or sold the furniture out of the house.

Sparky and Eileen were true lovebirds. He had perfect fingernails thanks to her.

Sparky was always trying to get Uncle Wayne to consider Chicks not just because Grandpa said to but because he was devoted to Chicks. Sparky talked like he ran Chicks when he never held a hammer or a wrench in his hand all his life. Sparky thought he was such a big shot. And Uncle Wayne would just laugh in his face.

So naturally Sparky was fit to be tied when one night Uncle Wayne called him up out of the blue and asked Do you think Chicks might be able to use someone on a temporary basis?

Sparky was in ecstasy. "Jesus, didn't I tell you they's dying over there for men with your expertise? I'll take this up with Mr. Chickowskowitz first thing in the morning!"

But what about California?
"Things has hit a snag."
But when was he going then?
"That isn't definite now."
But what does the Chief say?
Poor Uncle Wayne. You could feel his chagrin. He had to ask Mama if it was all right to stay. He had to ask Sparky about a job at Chicks. He'd spent all his money on that Chevy.

26

That night I heard Uncle Wayne pacing back and forth. I heard him kick my baseball bat across the room. I heard Mama call out to him from her bed. I heard him pacing.

When he came down in the morning I asked him why he couldn't just go to California now anyway and get a job out there, why couldn't he just stay with the Chief?

"Well that just don't happen to be the kind of arrangement I have with the man," Uncle Wayne said to me in a sarcastic singsong voice.

"Don't you even want to go to California anymore, Uncle Wayne?"

He sneered at me like I was a moron.

"Course I do. Not that it's any of your-type business."

Then he ambled away into the other room.

MAMA was fat. Her feet hurt so bad every day from waiting on tables and being fat the first thing she did when she got home at night was put them in a basin.

Below the hem of Mama's uniform skirt you could see the jelly rolls on her legs. Mama's arms filled out her sleeves. Under her cotton wrapper, Mama's haunches moved. Mama just ate and ate ever since Dad left.

I used to feel so sorry for Mama, pushing the carpet sweeper around on Saturdays and bending down to dust the table legs because no amount of screaming ever got the girls to help out.

Mama's pretty face had all but sunk out of sight. Yet someone fell in love with her.

He did not look like an ambulance-chaser but an undertaker for he dressed all in black save for his tan shoes like the plastic upholstery in a barbershop.

27

"That creep," Betty said. "You mean that creep came back today?"

Yes he came back when Mama was at home and listened sympathetically to her tale. Mama had never had anybody to tell everything to before Mr. Burrows.

She told him what I was wearing the night of my accident: corduroy pants with an elastic waist, a striped polo shirt, white socks, black oxford-style shoes.

Mr. Burrows wrote it all down and commented The white socks was a good detail. He urged Mama to omit nothing.

"We sat down to dinner anyway. I remember we was having chicken and string beans. I did not pour his milk yet. I remember my oldest girl said Isn't there any bread? For that's what I had sent him to the store for."

Here Mama stopped and blamed herself.

"Now," said Mr. Burrows.

Later Mama said "Oh I do not blame myself so much. I blame the carelessness of the child and the recklessness of that driver, who was going so fast in his truck on the curve."

"Did he have his headlights on, Mrs. McMullen?"

"Craig, did he have his headlights on?"

Did he have his headlights on? Did I see one single thing in the outside world before the truck chewed me up?

Mama was saying to Mr. Burrows "I guess talking about it has confused me."

She could be heard taking a deep breath.

"When the call came," Mama said, "I went to the hospital and the doctors told me what in their informed opinion had to be done. There wasn't any time. They put some papers under my nose and told me to sign them so I did. Did I do the right thing, Mr. Burrows?"

"I think you did fine, Mrs. McMullen."

28

I bet then he stared at her with his no-color eyes.

When Mama showed him to the door, Mr. Burrows said he knew it was no material comfort but there were many other souls in the world suffering through severe ordeals.

"Thank you so much," Mama said softly. "No one has ever bothered to say a word along that line before now."

Mama said we were going to get a million dollars and pay off all the terrible bills. How could she be so stupid as not to have found some lawyer before? Mama clapped her hands and got together all the papers, every scrap and REMINDER. Without Mr. Burrows even saying to she set about putting down her recollections. "Anything could count in my testimony," she said though she never had to testify. Fate sent Mr. Burrows to us, she said.

Uncle Sparky got into the act. He came back from downtown satisfied. "Your man has a two-room suite all his own, Janice."

"I knew he was a real lawyer," Mama sniffed, "but thank you anyway."

"Don't let him talk you into nothing but the very maximum however," counseled Sparky. "If you got the worm wet you may as well cast the hook in too."

"That poor child may never walk again," put in Aunt Eileen.

The first sign that anything was up came when the girls sat down for dinner one night and there were just two places at the table.

"Mama, you forgot a place—you forgot you."

"No I didn't."

"But look."

"No I didn't, Miss Smartypants, because I am eating out."

"You are?"

"Yes."

"Why?"

"Mr. Burrows is taking me out for catfish."

Mr. Burrows it seemed knew a place that had the best catfish. Mama happening to be a big catfish lover, he said he would take her out there, his treat. And this was long before any of his letters and threats started to bear fruit.

When Mama came home Delores asked "How was the catfish, Mama?" Her voice was full of insinuation.

"It was just delicious. What's that you think you're putting on your toenails?"

"It's called Tangerelo."

"Looks like mashed-up bugs to me."

"I think it's pretty. Didn't Mr. Burrows make a pass at you or anything, Mama?" Dolores thought she was so comic. "How many cocktails he make you drink?"

Mama came in and kissed me good-night—she'd had more than one cocktail, that's for sure. She left a waxy lipstick ring on my face and waltzed away upstairs.

I could see Dolores's foot up on the edge of the hassock with its green toenails and bits of cotton stuck between the toes.

"I bet Harold did it to you the very first time you went in his car," I said.

She did not say anything right away. Dolores was cool.

"I bet you let Harold do it to you a hundred times."

"Shut your hole," Dolores said but like she was the Good Fairy.

It soon was apparent, Mr. Burrows was not content with only company—he was serious about Mama. One day he even showed up at Monkey Wards. She saw him come in. He asked politely which her tables were then he sat down and had her serve him lunch. For a tip Mr. Burrows left a note that said

Good For One Dinner For Two At The River Queen and Movie

signed by him.

Soon Mama and Mr. Burrows were going together. He would take her to the Elks or for a drive to see the leaves. He would take her to a new movie every week. When Mama brought up the subject of weight, Mr. Burrows told her he felt some people did indeed have problems that can be accounted for by glands.

We only learned about Mr. Burrows in dribs and drabs—he was an orphan, for instance. Mama let that fall when Betty was complaining she had to share the bathroom.

"You could be like Mr. Burrows," Mama said. "He had to share a bathroom with seventy other boys in his orphanage, not just one older sister."

Mr. Burrows never had family of any kind and maybe that explained a little the great interest he took in ours.

How did I feel having only sisters, he asked when he was waiting for Mama to come down one night. Did I miss brothers? Did I ever get lonely for some? Did I ever wish it was only me and Mama? What did I think about Grandpa? Mr. Burrows said he'd heard Grandpa was some remarkable fella.

Mr. Burrows would pull up a straight-backed chair and sit with one leg crossed over his knee, a cigarette sputtering between his fingers, and he would quiz me.

Did I know where talcum powder came from? Did I ever read Washington Irving's Headless Horseman? Did I know the Russians were going to put a man on the moon before us? What made tears?

I guess Mr. Burrows thought all this education was going to qualify him to be my dad.

"What if we get him for a father?" I asked Betty.

"Yuck, that cretin?"

I asked Betty what a cretin was and she said "That's for me to know and you to find out but." Then she made some ugly faces. "Let me just say this, if Mr. Burrows marries Mama I am going to commit double suicide."

Imagine having Mr. Burrows for a dad! It would be like living at a funeral. He would always be around licking his teeth and posing questions.

But Mama admired him so. "Look what that poor orphan

31

boy did on his own. A person can do anything," she said. "Things do not, my boy, come to him who waits."

I was waiting but only for my limb.

"SEIZE LIFE!" said the preacher on TV. "SEIZE LIFE! TAKE LIFE IN THY HANDS! SMELL OF ITS FRAGRANCE!"

WITHOUT me other boys were picking out their lockers. Without me they were breaking the spines on their books, having fistfights, giving cherry-bellies. Without me other boys were carving big tits on the desktops.

So that fall Betty came home all hot and bothered because at school one of the cheerleaders had to drop out. They picked the cheerleaders in the spring so the girls could perfect their routines in the summer, but that year one of them had to drop out and to Betty this was her big chance.

In the spring when she was still in junior high she had taken the bus across town for weeks to the high school to learn the cheers. But that time she lost and cried her eyes out. Betty was Captain in her junior high and everybody knew cheerleader was the best a girl could be.

Mama only said At least you now know how to get to the high school, I hope it gets you farther than it did Dolores.

But then when one of the cheerleaders had to drop out our house trembled again under Betty's high-kicks and stomps. She practiced yelling but under her breath "Pushemback, pushemback, waaaaaaaayback!" and spent more hours at the gym where the cheerleaders once more gave lessons to every pretty girl in school.

When the morning of the big tryout came Betty was up early

doing cheers in our living room. Dolores came down in a sweater and the pointy bra she favored since she met Harold.

"You'll never get it. I don't know why you're knocking yourself out."

"Heyhey whadayasay getheballinfight!"

"You don't have allure."

Last period of that day, all the pretty girls in the school sat in their classes a mess of nerves waiting for the cheerleaders to come around and call on just one of them, take her out in the hall and pin on the mum with the tell-tale megaphone with her name.

It was Betty.

"I never thought I would get it but I'm so glad I did!"

They took Betty down to the girl's locker room and picked out a letter sweater for her and a skirt then took her to the drugstore for a soda.

"Seriously," the head cheerleader said silencing the giggles, "it is a bunch of hard work, Betty. The glamour wears off very quick. But there's one thing we wanted to say to you—it came out in the voting. I hope you don't mind but we feel you should get a pixie cut. All that hair is just going to get in your way and nothing's worse than a wet ponytail."

So Betty needed a new haircut. She needed a lot of things all of a sudden—boys were already calling up for dates. She needed most of all to buy a pair of those saddle-shoes. That was what the cheerleaders wore.

The problem was, during football season games were held on Saturdays and Betty was working at Woolworths. "If you quit Woolworths," Mama said, "how you going to pay for all those white crew socks and lipstick?"

"Mama I have to quit Woolworths or I can't be a cheerleader!"

Betty cried and cried because Mama was going to make her work in the dimestore. She could not move Mama so she talked the girl's gym teacher into helping her with a loan for the shoes and she got Woolworths to let her work two nights after school so it all worked out, but she hated Mama for this.

Now she would only talk to Mama when she had to—"Yes, Mother," she would say.

I would hear her on the phone. "That's all right," she would say. "I'll meet you there, no really, let me meet you there." She never once asked a boy to our house.

Why didn't Mama notice—Dolores never had boys to our house either. If you listened to Dolores, you would have thought Poor her, she had never had a date all year.

Dolores slunk in and out. According to Dolores, she did all her homework in study hall. Anyway, she liked to quote Mama as saying, they never hold you back two years running.

Mama was acting like she was almost in love with Mr. Burrows. Maybe she was sincerely. I know she loved the attention Mr. Burrows paid her.

He even drove her to Warren one Saturday. He said he was going over that way and he wondered if she would like to pay a visit to her folks. Put that way, it did not seem like she was introducing him to them and she said yes. But in the back of Mama's mind must have been that Mr. Burrows would meet them.

"I'll drop you off and come back by after I've completed my business in Beaver Crossing," he said.

"Can't you come in?"

"Well if you don't think that would be an intrusion."

"Oh William, you don't know my folks."

Mr. Burrows trembled before Grandpa but on the way back to Lincoln he observed that Grandpa was of the old school.

Mama said Grandpa sometimes put people off.

Mr. Burrows apologized for himself though. "I am not always so adroit in a social setting."

Could Mama marry Mr. Burrows and go to bed with him?

Betty made vomit sounds when we talked about it. Mama knew how not to have any more kids—even though she was a convert to Catholicism she was not a good one. One thing was for sure, no one had ever turned to Mama, as Mr. Burrows did in his car, and said about Grandpa "He is of the old school."

To Mama, that summed Grandpa up. Someone had at last found words that made him bigger and smaller at the same time.

For a while here, then, it looked like everyone was in love in our house. Mama was in love with Mr. Burrows. Betty since she made cheerleader was in love with herself. Dolores was so in love with Harold she acted like a thief night and day.

Dolores used to lie to people she met and say she was really an Indian—"I have part-Apache blood." She was not pretty. Her feet were too big—this was the kind of thing she talked about constantly. But she said she was going to overcome her defects. She read magazines and wore perfume. She combed her hair over one eye and she would then toss back her head smiling in the mirror.

She never wanted to be a girl—she always wanted to be a woman even when she was little. When she was little for Christmas she prayed for a purse on a chain with rouge and a powder puff inside and a plastic pretend lipstick that went up and down like a red bullet. She walked around the house in Mama's high heels and when she got bigger she still walked up on her toes to give an impression of poise.

Suddenly men were turning on the street and going "va-va-voom" at her and she started wearing a black ribbon around her neck.

Now she was leading two lives with Harold like a Communist spy. She was so good. She came and went with downcast eyes.

But one day Betty found written in curlicues all over Dolores' notebook paper

HAROLD HAROLD HAROLD
Harold XXX
H.S.
Mrs. H.S.
Mrs. Dolores Stavrinos
Dee Stavrinos
Delilah St. S

Far from wanting to snitch, Betty entered into her secret just like me.

"And all this time I didn't know!" Betty sounded like someone discovering a floorwax on TV.

"If you say one word to Mama I will kill you."

"Cross my heart no!"

Before Dolores, Betty oozed sympathy for the star-crossed lovers but with me she was a two-faced weasel.

"God, can you imagine," she said to me. "Harold! Harold is uh-glee!"

Uncle Wayne and his friends called Harold the Geek because he was a Greek and he was so ugly. "Harold is uh-glee!" they would say to his face. Harold was the Geek. Martin was Martino. Butchy was Butchy. Uncle Wayne was Spike. These were their nicknames.

"Harold is uh-glee!" Betty got giddy, doubled over.

"Harold is a toad," I said. "Harold is like a toad in the road. Harold is like a squished old horn toad!"

"Harold is like a squished horn toad the car ran over!" Betty shrieked falling onto the foot of my bed. "Ugh! I would never let Harold touch me for anything."

I laughed until my ribs hurt. We would stop then start again. But in spite of our laughter, we both knew the way you can close your eyes and bring your two fingertips together—Dolores was going to get herself knocked up.

THE first day on the job at Chicks, Sparky took Uncle Wayne all over the place one hand glued to his back so everyone could see who got Wayne the job.

"Course neptunism isn't company policy here, howsomever," Sparky hee-hawed to the men at every work station.

At Chicks they put Uncle Wayne in charge of three machines on the line. His foreman was named Rodney and Rodney was greatly admired. When Sparky took Wayne up to meet Rodney, Rodney said "You mean he ain't seven foot tall with ten arms? Well maybe he's got Einstein's brain in there anyway as you say he does, Sparky."

Rodney told Uncle Wayne that first day "A man should know his machine so he can do one thing superbly so I would like you to just take your time here getting acquainted."

Uncle Wayne learned fast. Soon he knew his job backwards and forward. He buckled down for he was saving up to buy that garage with the Chief. Soon he was promoted to trouble-shooter.

But this didn't seem to be enough for Uncle Wayne. He worked a forty-hour week at Chicks then got him a moonlighting job pumping gas too. We just figured he was waiting for that snag in California to come undone.

Every night Uncle Wayne came home so beat. He ate his dinner and went to his other job or upstairs to his bed. He yelled at the girls. He did not horse around anymore or joke with me.

37

* * *

When he saw that letter his eyebrows shot up. He held that letter between two fingers.

Uncle Wayne's hands were black under the nails. His fingerprints could be read from the ground-in grease. His nose was flecked with blackheads. He was getting like his machines, greasy and dark. Uncle Wayne was powerful. His body was well-honed. He could lift up a car by the bumper. For a small man his shoulders were broad. His arms were ropey. His wrists worked like ball bearings. He had that AIR MAIL letter in his hand then he put it in his breast pocket and sat down to dinner.

He ate pinto beans with cornbread. The only time he said a word was to ask for more. Feeding Uncle Wayne was like throwing gasoline onto a fire—Mama piled up the cornbread and the beans. Uncle Wayne took three helpings with lots of ketchup. Then he ate two dishes of cling peaches. Meanwhile he drank two bottles of beer.

He belched and pushed back his chair. He stretched and touched that letter in his breast pocket then he went upstairs to read it.

At three A.M. the Highway Patrol brought Uncle Wayne to our door the way they used to bring Dad.

They told Mama he was lucky they didn't put him in jail. They told her the location of his Chevy.

He had thrown up the beans all over himself. Mama made him take off his clothes at the front door.

"They have got me," Uncle Wayne said. "They have got me again."

"No they do not," Mama said. "They let you go this time."

"No they have got me."

The next day Uncle Wayne went to work late and shook so bad Rodney took him off the line. He was so sick Rodney sent him home. When Sparky saw Uncle Wayne walking across the

38

parking lot through the office window, he ran outside like a shot.

Uncle Wayne was struggling to get into his car.

"Got the bug, huh?" said Sparky through the window.

Uncle Wayne just drove off.

When I was little Dad used to sit in his chair and let me climb on him. I used to climb up on Dad's shoe and hold onto his leg. I used to flop over his knee and walk all over him. I used to sit on Dad's shoulders and hold onto his ears. I used to play Mountain on Dad.

But when Dad got tired of Mountain he would give me his beer to drink. He would put his hat on my head. I would stagger around the room until I fell down.

Then Dad would cry What have I done? and bawl. Dad would grab me and squeeze the wind out of me. He would beg forgiveness.

Mama would come home and I would be asleep drunk on the living room floor. Dolores told me this.

Uncle Wayne's friends did not notice the change after he got that letter. Uncle Wayne's friends thought he was the same old Wayne. They thought he was funny. It was just like old times to them.

One night at the Big Top he got beat up by some lady's boyfriend. One other night his friends brought Uncle Wayne home with panties on his head.

"I really got to apologize," said Harold to Mama when they had got Wayne upstairs. "They's quite adolescent."

So Uncle Wayne went downhill like a monkey on a greased pole and I watching from my bed saw him crawl up the stairs like Dad used to on his hands and knees nights and I decided I must hate him.

THE County said "You don't get this boy into rehabilitative therapy, he'll never walk without pain. Now I'm here to tell you, you don't I'm going to file a report. And why the dickens didn't you wean him off these painkillers when you were told?"

Mama was shook. No one ever had told her she was a bad mother before and here she was only waiting for Mr. Burrows to get us our settlement. She didn't mean to turn me into some kind of dope fiend. When the doctor left she cried and took away my pills.

I was so sick Mama called up the doctor. "I followed your instructions to the letter but, doctor, can't we give him nothing, he's sweating so heavy, I'm scared."

I heard Dad outside on the lawn, the click-clip of his hedge clippers. The hand on my forehead was on the end of a long rubber arm like the cable of a bridge running up to Uncle Wayne's eyes.

But soon I would have a limb.

TEENAGE YOUTH WINS SWIMMING MEDAL

Everyone today was talking about Craig McMullen, the boy who has won the Gold Medal swimming contest here in Paris with only one leg, incredible as that may sound. The teenager from Lincoln bested all others in the difficult finals. His mother Janice, also of Lincoln, and two sisters, older than him, are flying over to meet the young hero, who is also a track star, in the President's jet plane.

40

Soon they would let me into physical therapy so I could learn how to walk again.

"But you won't be able to go back to school," said Dolores.

"Why not?"

"They don't take cripples there."

I told Wesley I would not exactly have my new limb but I would have a temporary—this is what I was hoping. Wesley looked sideways at my stump. He had never asked to see it, not until the night he slept over and we made our tent.

I was pleading with Mama to let me have Wesley sleep over as we used to before my accident.

"That was then," she always said.

"But this is a big enough bed, Mama."

"I know it is."

"Why was it then then?"

"Because it was."

But finally Mama said we could. "No he don't have something," I heard her say over the phone. "He's perfectly okay. He's like any boy too you know."

So Wesley got to come over one night with his p.j.s in a paper bag and his toothbrush. He brought his mess kit from the Scouts as well—this mess kit came in an olive-drab slipcover and contained a frying pan and a plate, a collapsible cup, knife, fork and spoon, all out of aluminum.

Wesley regaled me with tales of scouting. He told me about his first overnight hike. They cooked a meal, he said, and ate it out of their mess kits. They cooked the potatoes in foil in the fire and the beans in the can so you wondered why people even bothered to take them out and put them in a pan.

> Beans, beans the musical fruit
> The more you eat the more you toot

41

The more you toot the better you feel
So eat your beans at every meal

They waded in a crick and studied underwater life. They hiked at least fifty miles.

This gave us the idea for the tent. So Mama let us string up a rope from one nail to the window and hang two sheets over it with clothes pins. Then we needed a flashlight. What do you need that for, said Mama, if you got on the TV? For late at night, I said. In case any of us needs to take a whiz-bang in the bushes, whispered Wesley.

We watched TV till Mama made us turn it off and said Go asleep. Then Wesley told me more about scouting. You had to learn the Morris code—he tapped some on the rail for me with his knife until Mama yelled downstairs.

The knots held up a lot of boys, Wesley said, though not him since he was so proficient at knots because his Dad helped him every Sunday after church. In scouting you have to promise to do your best to do your duty and dig a latrine to do it in, Wesley said. That cracked me up. Everything Wesley said that night cracked me up.

I was so happy. It was Indian summer. The windows were open and our tent was cozy with the glow of the flashlight so weak Wesley had to keep shaking the batteries inside to keep it going.

In scouting after dinner after everyone scrubbed out his mess kit with sand and rinsed it in the crick, you sang songs and told ghost stories "But they're such baby stuff I won't tell you any" then you went into your tent and slept in a sleeping bag.

"Here we are in our tent!"

"Yes," Wesley said, "but it's sooooooo dark out there camping out. Bats and bears. Every little noise. Some kids can't even go asleep their first night. You think they'd never been camping."

"Yeah," I said.

". . . So the salesman comes back five years later and there's this little kid out in the yard. He's real skinny. And the salesman says Boy, are you skinny, and the little kid says You'd be skinny too if you was strained through a sheet."

"I guess we ought to go asleep," Wesley said at length. "I guess it's getting pretty late."

"Tell another one, Wesley."

"I can't remember any more."

We lay quiet at the end of the night I never wanted to end. The bed was like a raft afloat on the dark sea—the batteries in the flashlight were dead for good. It started raining outside our tent, breaking out like goose bumps, falling on the fallen leaves in the yard.

Wesley's voice was small in the dark. When I turned to him I could see the whites of his eyes over there on the pillow.

"Could I feel your leg?"

I was surprised. All that night long Wesley had still looked away when he was liable to catch a glimpse of even my empty p.j. leg.

I said "If you want to."

"I won't hurt it."

"I know that."

"I just want to see what it feels like."

So I rolled my p.j. leg up over the stump and let him feel the bandage.

"Does it hurt?"

"Uh-uh."

He felt around a bit more. "What's it really like?"

So I took down my p.j.s in the dark and unwound the bandage, which I was not supposed to do. I lay back. Wesley patted around on the mattress until he hit it then his hand shot away.

43

I heard him swallow. His hand then floated back over here and rested on the stump.

"It's like anything," he said.

"It's just flesh and blood."

"It's bumpy."

He felt it.

"It's a little soft but for these lines, like a baby's head."

"I never thought of that," I said, feeling myself. "It is somewhat."

Wesley lay back on his pillow. I wrapped up my stump as best I could. I pulled on my pants.

"I just wanted to see," he said.

"I know."

"That didn't hurt?"

We lay there. My heart started beating. There came a singing in my head. I could feel the heat from Wesley next to me. My dick was standing up against my p.j. pants.

Wesley must have thought I was ashamed of my stump, I was so quiet. Maybe he regretted asking. But all of a sudden he turned over on his side with his back to me and pulled his knees up against his chest.

I listened to the rain outside our tent.

"Wesley?"

When he answered it was like I was rousing him but I could tell he was still wide awake.

"Wesley, you think I can feel your dick?"

After considering, I guess, he said yes. His voice was breathy. He turned over on his back. He pulled down his pants and turned to me. He pointed it at me. I stroked the top with my fingers and watched it get hard.

"Me too."

But Wesley jerked up in bed and shushed me.

We froze, listening hard. We listened.

"She's asleep," I whispered. "Honest."

Wesley hunched back down. His dick was now limp again but mine was poking out through the slit in my p.j.s.

Wesley then said I don't think we should and pulled up his pants.

"Come on." The skin on mine felt like it would bust.

"It isn't right."

"Sure it is."

"Not for a Baptist."

"Didn't you do it, Wesley? Didn't you do it once with me?"

"Once I did it with you."

"Well, I bet other boys do it in the Scouts."

"I bet they don't!"

"I bet they do."

Wesley must have known that was true for he could only repeat It isn't right.

"Sure it is."

"No it isn't."

Then I was inspired to say "They even do it in the navy. My Uncle Wayne told me. You don't think they have girls on ships, do you? They have to get rid of their jizz on ships too. If they don't it impairs performance." I was talking so fast I was almost out of breath. I wanted to roll over on top of Wesley. "Let me do it to you first then," I said. "If you don't like it, well you don't have to do it to me."

"I don't believe that ship stuff," Wesley said.

"My Uncle Wayne told me, Wesley. He even showed me how."

"Liar."

"He did. Lots and lots of times."

"Liar."

"He showed me the best way. Wanna see?"

"You're lying and they don't do that in Scouts either."

I couldn't get Wesley to. I even reached over and felt around there but he let me for only a minute then pushed my hand

45

away. He turned over on his side again. I said "Mama's fast asleep, Wesley, she never wakes up" but he would not answer. He pretended to go asleep.

Of course I had been doing this to myself all along—Mama didn't know that because I'd learned to hold it in.

I thought that night about doing it to myself in spite of Wesley being there. I thought about asking him if he minded but I didn't. What I really wanted more, I knew, was to feel Wesley's hand on it the way I had before.

Late, late I heard Uncle Wayne come in but I couldn't see how drunk he was that night on account of our tent. Wesley stirred in his sleep when the door slammed shut.

I felt ashamed for telling those lies about the navy and Uncle Wayne. Shame burned on my face. Then I remembered I was supposed to hate Uncle Wayne now.

DOLORES thought she could marry Harold without confessing to Mama—it was hard enough to get him to say he would. She waited until after Thanksgiving to tell.

"I am the happiest woman in the world," she announced to Mama.

"What does Harold say?" Mama spoke softly.

"What do you mean? Mama, I said we're getting married."

Mama hit her hard. Then while Dolores sat on the floor crying Mama walked back and forth figuring out aloud how this happened and what she was going to do about it.

She grabbed Dolores by the hair. "You are, aren't you! Aren't you!"

Dolores admitted, she was p.g. "But it was an accident!"

That made Mama drop her hands. Dolores's sobs grew fewer and farther between. For a while she tried to keep it up but then she must have thought, considering, she got off pretty easy.

"Can't I go get a Kleenex?"

So Dolores snuffled and sniffed and got up off the floor and went upstairs and blew her nose. This was always how it was. Dolores would do something bad. Mama would hit her. There would be harsh words. Five minutes later Dolores would be outside playing.

When she came down Mama told her to sit next to her on the couch. She took Dolores' hand and laced their fingers together.

"How long is it?"

"Since? I haven't had you know what for two months."

"Uh-huh."

"I would of known."

Mama nodded. She tried to think of anything anyone ever told her about this—when Dolores was little they lived up above a lady people said got rid of babies for you. Mama thought at that time how happy she was she didn't do that to Dolores.

She could only remember what her own mama had said to her in a situation just like this one:

"But why did you marry without telling us?"

"But that's not what I'm saying, Mama. Listen. I'm trying to say we are not married but I am going to have a baby."

"You are not married? But you're going to have a baby aren't you?"

Now Mama asked Dolores, "Do his folks know?"

Dolores spoke like things were perfectly normal. "Not yet, we thought we would tell you first, Mama." Visions of wedding bells danced in Dolores' head.

"Harold is seven years older than you. And what makes you think he will stand by his pledge?"

47

"Why not? Why wouldn't he?" Dolores was suspicious now that Mama might snatch him away.

Mama took her time speaking in a calm voice and conjured up a long struggle and Dolores alone p.g. in the world at the end of which Dolores cried "But he loves me!" and fled from the room.

In the end Mama got stumped. She didn't know what to do. She felt she should be dead set against this but what about that baby then?

So they were wed.

Dolores had her way in almost everything. She had two bridesmaids dressed in the same color, pink—Betty was one making one of her faces. Dolores insisted on a church wedding even if Mama had said A quiet one. The happy couple received many presents from the groom's people including a new set of luggage for their postponed honeymoon since Harold had to work.

After the wedding everyone came to our house for cake and ice cream. Harold's folks didn't yet know the truth. They thought ugly Harold was so lucky. They never expected anyone would ever want to marry Harold. In gratitude Harold's folks presented the newlyweds with a trailer home.

At this party Uncle Wayne got real drunk and took Harold out on the front porch and yelled at him. "You cradle-robbing motherfucker," he yelled. "You don't treat this little girl right I'll nail your balls to the wall."

Harold tried to laugh it off but his two brothers separated them.

On the day of the wedding Mama did not just have to pretend she was happy, she was. The day before Mr. Burrows had dropped by to announce his out-of-court settlement of ten-thousand-five-hundred dollars for my accident. Mr. Burrows was now officially our savior.

"You thank Mr. Burrows when he comes out of the bathroom. We are going to buy you the best leg!"

48

"Don't worry," Betty told me. "She will have a tough time marrying Mr. Burrows. She first would have to find Dad."

So lo and behold, two weeks later when Dolores is all settled into that trailer and the bad news is broke to Harold's folks, she gets a card in the mail at our house. It has a silver foil bell on the front and inside it is signed

Your Dad

You can just make out the postmark. It says DENVER COLO.

DAD was in Denver. We now knew this and Mama called up Uncle Bill and screamed at him for lying, he knew where Dad was all the time, but Uncle Bill just said lots of people read the home-town paper.

I only thought Please God I hope Dad stays out of our hair.

I was going to go to school again. I was going to get my limb. I was going to be happy for a change.

Dad was in Denver building himself a new house. His name in Denver was Louis J. MacKnight and he worked for a construction firm where he was considered their most valuable asset.

When it was all over, Dad's neighbors said he was a quiet solitary man who never bothered a living soul and they could not understand. In the summer they would see Dad packing the car to go up fishing in the mountains. He wore a fishing hat with lures on it. In the winter they would see Dad out shoveling the sidewalks—holding back the kitchen curtains the wives would remark How vigorous Mr. MacKnight is, Dear, he never seems to sit still. The husbands would call out Take it easy, you're

49

gonna bust a vessel! from their front steps but Dad just laughed and kept on shoveling and shoveled their walks too.

For a renter, Dad sure did keep a property up. He trimmed his trees and edged his grass. He gave the lawn a good soak on alternate odd/even days during rationing. He put out bulbs in the fall when who knew if he would be there to see them come up in the spring?

Dad's new house was rising on an acre of land west of Denver almost in the foothills. Dad was already planning his landscaping—lots of dwarf fruit trees he thought, and hedges, little wire fences along the borders, a rock garden and bird-bath someday. Dad was building himself a split-level with a two-car garage on it. He was building it himself almost without any help. He had already raised the chimney laying all the bricks himself. Dad knew so much about everything.

What there was of Dad's house stood all alone in the dirt. There wasn't anything around it. The sewers were in and the poles were up but no one yet had built there but Dad. Now it is solid houses for miles and miles.

Everyone liked Dad. No one knew him. They did not know anything about his past—he had a story all made up that he never got to use. He did not socialize. He did not bowl or go to baseball games. He did not even have a TV. But Dad was a churchgoer. Three times a week he attended a church called the Circle of Holiness that met in people's houses. Dad was Born Again.

Because Dad had almost died. One day in Texas he fell off a girder onto his head. There was no way he could have, for Dad was totally unconscious, but he saw himself laying there and the men kneeling around him opening up his shirt and yelling Don't move him!

As if from on high, Dad hovered over his prone body. He floated up there in a halo of light. A hand dropped onto his shoulder. It was God.

50

ARE YOU READY SON

Oh, just let me watch a while!

Dad said.

The ambulance came and they put Dad on a stretcher. He thought he would die in the ambulance and they said later they thought he did.

IT IS TIME

said his heavenly father.

Let me watch just a little bit more!

Dad begged like someone who wants to watch the movie all the way through a second time.

"I don't know what the hell to do for him," said the doctor in the emergency room. So he didn't do anything.

So they put Dad in a bed in traction so he couldn't move an inch and he lived.

IT IS PAST TIME SON

Please just a minute!

Then the hand of God withdrew from Dad's shoulder and its warmth receded. God turned away from Dad in resignation.

So Dad spent all his Sundays now praying and praising the Lord and studying what He said in the Bible. Dad gave one-tenth of all his income to God. He had not had a drop of booze for three years. He kept his own counsel with God's benevolent assistance.

Dad's whole previous life, he now saw, was a long valley of tears where he gave but heartbreak to each one he came into contact with. He had worshipped the false idols of greed and sensual pleasure and now Dad felt he had been granted the earned gift of a whole new life to make up for that. He hoped he could prove worthy. He tried and looked for a way to pay back God.

Other boys were tumbling and summersaulting and turning cartwheels. They were climbing ropes and swarming over the monkey bars. They were swinging on the rings. I myself was creeping between those walking bars and down that rubber mat.

When I started my physical therapy I had muscles like Jell-O from being in that bed too long and sores up and down my backside. When I started it hurt so bad I would say to myself Why live if this is life? I didn't know this happens to everyone sooner or later. I was a mere child. Not even seeing the struggles of those less fortunate than I was made me feel at that point you should live any more than you should not.

But soon, I kept telling myself, you will have your own blue notebook back with the three-hole paper and your pencil box with the ship flags on it and inside the right number of pencils, a little sharpener for the one you lost, your three-color ballpoint and the pink eraser that works on ink too.

If Mama now had all that money for my rehabilitation, she still let the County pay for what I got. And if she ever shed a tear for my pain she shed it in private maybe because she thought it would deter my progress if I knew.

When I did finally go back to school it was in Warren, not Lincoln, and it was to the sixth grade. I didn't know anyone. I was on two sticks. I was older than all the other children. No one was my friend.

And from being a boy who was not ever noticed in school, I became the one who was always noticed but in a new way—no one would so much as look in my direction even if my affliction was not visible. Somehow just knowing it was there made it worse. I was shunned. I was called names behind my back.

I myself had done this to other children. I myself had folded up paper into cooty-catchers to torment less fortunate children and when the teacher said we must be kind I had paid no attention to her.

DOLORES and Harold were so happy in their little trailer. They almost forgot they were going to have a baby—they were so pleased not to have to sneak around anymore it was like they were going steady for the first time.

Dolores liked being able to come and go when she wanted without answering to anyone but her beloved. She could go down the road to the store for a coke at any time. She liked being Harold's wife, she told us, for now it seemed he cherished her more. Now that he was responsible for both of them totally, she said, he acted more like a man. Oh, he would clown around—when she did something stupid he would pretend to strangle her to death and they would both laugh.

At first she made a few stabs at fixing up the trailer, but soon she gave up. It was a lost cause, and anyway they would soon be in their house. For now Dolores and Harold could be as slobby as they wanted so there were clothes and magazines laying all over the place and the ashtrays overflowed. It got worse when Dolores got bigger and bigger. Even just mopping the little strip of linoleum in front of her sink seemed too much for her. Harold would come home and say "Dee, what did I marry you for anyway?"

But their passion for each other did not cool and this is what they were doing when the phone rang that night. It rang six or seven times before Harold picked it up.

So at ten the next morning Harold was down at the jail when they brought Uncle Wayne back from court. Harold had to wait an hour or so before Wayne could come out into the hall.

"You got a cigarette?"

Harold shook one out for him. Wayne looked bad. That night before Harold had asked over the phone What's the matter, Spike, you drunk again? but Wayne did not chuckle, only said I wish to hell I was.

Wayne walked right through the revolving doors. Outside on the steps Harold asked "What's up?" but Wayne didn't answer.

When Harold unlocked the passenger side Wayne slipped into the car. He was holding his hands as prisoners do to show you how harmless they are. He sat with his hands in his lap while Harold walked around the car. He took a long drag on the cigarette and the smoke spread out on the windshield.

Harold got in behind the wheel. He'd thought all this would be jocular but now he was worried.

"This thing out of gas?" Wayne said.

Harold turned the key. The car rattled in the cold then started.

"You didn't say where to."

Wayne just sneered and looked out the side window.

So Harold started out for our house. They drove in silence down the icy streets. Harold wondered if it was aggravated assault—it must be something bad. But Wayne didn't look like he'd been in a fight. His clothes were clean and his face unmarked. He just looked like shit.

"What was it, Spike?"

"Huh?"

Harold pulled over to the curb and stopped the car. He

54

turned off the motor. They were not halfway to our house. Wayne looked around.

"Listen, buddy, I just shelled out one-hundred dollars up there. What the fuck's going on?" Harold's voice sounded weak and frightened to him.

Wayne then spoke to Harold like he was some snot-nosed kid. "Harold, just drive me home, I ain't slept a wink, you hear?"

That night when Harold saw Wayne's name in the paper he laughed his ass off.

What a colossal error, he said to himself.

Nevertheless he remembered Wayne had not seen any humor in what happened to him. If he had, he would have told Harold all about it, wouldn't he? Harold did not show the item to his precious Dolores.

P ERHAPS if he had not found out about it the way he did Sparky would not have made it worse. But when he came into work that morning Denning motioned him into his office.

"You better sit down," Denning said.

Alarmed, Sparky did—Denning never had him in his office, preferring handwritten notes.

Denning took a newspaper clipping out of his shirt pocket.

Now Denning didn't like Wayne. Sparky knew this. Denning called Wayne a fuck-up in front of Mr. Chickowskowitz. He did because one of Wayne's machines down on the floor was sending up clouds of smoke so Sparky could not very well contradict Denning at the time but later he took him aside.

"Jesus, Bob, can't you let up in front of Mr. Chick? This

55

guy's my brother-in-law and I brought him in here, you know."

"Yeah?" Denning said. "You seem to forget from time to time, I'm the personnel man here. So I suppose that makes you the monkey's uncle, don't it?"

Now Sparky read the newspaper clipping all the way through but he didn't get it. It made him a little sick to his stomach but he didn't get it.

"So?"

Denning was perched on his desk. He smiled.

Sparky started to read it all the way through again then his eyes darted down to the line

W. Smith, Resident of Lincoln

and the hairs stood up on his neck. He read the first two or three paragraphs again. He wiped his mouth with the back of his hand and glanced up at Denning. Then he handed the clipping back.

"Can't be," Sparky croaked.

"Tis."

"Can't be."

Denning seemed to sigh and picked up a file folder with Wayne's name neatly inked on it. Sparky was sitting back in the leather chair like a jet pilot in a plane taking off. Denning reached into the file and pulled out a piece of paper with a printed seal on the top. He held it before Sparky's eyes.

Sparky read this too. He read this twice too. It was confirmation of Uncle Wayne's discharge from the navy. It said

DISHONORABLE

"Son of a bitch." Sparky could not think how to save himself from this. Wayne had lied to him and to everybody. He must have been forcibly separated from the navy, not just decided he wasn't going to sign up again. "Holy jumping shit."

"And now," said Denning from a certain distance, "I'd like

you to tell me what it says in this little box down here," pointing.

Sparky read the box then he looked up at Denning with baby-blue eyes.

"Why?" Sparky said when Denning didn't answer.

"So?" Sparky said.

"Not being the personnel officer around here," said Denning, "you did not send for this confirmation form, did you? Being the personnel officer who is acquainted with such matters I did. And not being the personnel officer why would you have any reason to know this is a code?" Only then did Denning raise his voice. "I never would of hired that fuck-up of a brother-in-law of yours in the first place and not just because he's a drunkard. You know why in addition?"

Goddamnit, Sparky thought.

"Now look here, Bob, this man here's been a damned good worker."

"Cocksucker," Denning said.

At first Sparky thought Denning meant him.

"This code means the man's a cocksucker," said Denning pointing to it like he held the patent on it. "That's what this code means, chum."

IT could be any Smith, see?"

"But it ain't."

"Honey, it could be any Smith. Lincoln is full of Smiths, see? There's two pages of Smiths in the phone book, Honey. There's lots of Smiths here. Wallace Smith, Wilbert Smith, two William Smiths. Look!"

"Can't."

Sparky lay on the bed. His shoes were still on his feet. The ice-bag over his eye was almost water.

"Well what did he say, Honey?"

"He wasn't caught up in no dragnet if that's what you mean."

"But what was he doing there?"

"He was in there with the rest of em."

Aunt Eileen was still in her robe—she'd hardly expected Sparky back home in the middle of the day.

It traveled like wildfire around the factory but Wayne turned his back and went on working. He didn't know what else to do. Then Sparky got hysterical when he wouldn't leave so he had to hit him.

They will have to fire me proper, Wayne said to himself. No one fires me from a job just like that—though in truth he had been fired from the navy just like that and his commanding officer was not able to restrain himself from yelling at him after the court martial.

So at three o'clock Rodney finally walks up and hands Wayne his pink slip and says It would be a good idea if you leave now before the end of the shift.

They stood amidst the whir and pounding of the machines. Wayne had to shout. "And what if I don't?" But Rodney's face was filled with hatred and that as much as anything else prompted Wayne to turn and go.

Aunt Eileen lay on the bed with Sparky. "Not my baby brother," she said. "No."

Sparky had explained the evidence to her three times at least. "No no no."

Then Sparky was up, putting on his jacket.

"Where you going? Don't go out asking for more trouble, Honey!"

Sparky kissed her on the hair.

"I am not going out asking for any trouble."
Sparky looked almost jaunty with that eye.
"Then where are you going?"
"To Monkey Wards before your sister gets off work."

Wayne went right to the nearest bar. After a couple of shots he felt better. He said to himself he would assess his situation calmly. He said to himself he would stand back and take the measure of it. Problem was, his damned hand was shaking so bad he could barely light a cigarette. Well, the worst had happened. Ha! The worst just kept on.

When Mama came out of work there was Sparky at the elevator.

"Thought I'd drive you home," he said taking her by the arm. He punched the button for the elevator.

"You get the day off?" was the first thing she thought of saying. Mama imagined Sparky downtown all day looking in all the shop windows, buying himself underwear. "What happened to your eye?"

He didn't answer. They went down in the elevator. He still had her arm.

"What's wrong? Is it Craig?"

For Sparky he was being downright breezy. Whistling a tune softly he walked her out of the building. He held open his car door for her.

When he got in the other side she asked "Is this some kind of surprise?" She was briefly flustered, like a Queen for a Day.

But Sparky would not answer. He drove them to the city park. He stopped next to the duck pond and turned to her. By this time Mama was hopping mad.

He never once thought about not telling her.

59

*   *   *

Lincoln police today reported that 7 men were apprehended last night for lewd and lascivious behavior at the municipal bus depot.

District Attorney Madison Schultz affirmed that the bust was in response to numerous complaints to his office that the men's rest room at the station was the scene of vice.

Decent citizens and travelers could not use the facility due to this other element, said the D.A. Police and his office worked together, he said.

D.A. Schultz released the men's names to the press in hopes, he said, that "it will serve warning on others of their kind."

Apprehended in the raid were:

P. Codd, Resident of Lincoln

F. David, Resident of Chicago, Ill.

S. Galvin, Resident of Lincoln

K. Notes, No Address

W. Olmstead, Resident of Cedar Bluffs

W. Smith, Resident of Lincoln

J. M. Yelland, Resident of Lincoln

THE Chief's letter warned him

They have some way of knowing. It has not just been my imagination.

Now Wayne knew he was right. It was not just the DISHONORABLE on his discharge or else even with the whole fucking world knowing he could go out and find another job where there wasn't a Denning to give a shit.

He knew on account of Sparky the Chief was right, there is something on their forms.

This made him despair in a way he had not yet even when the Chief wrote the letter which cast him off.

We would both be hounded across the face of the earth by this.

They had not just bored holes in the wall at the bus station, they had bored right into his life.

Wayne knew now he was one. He'd gone ahead and been it on his own without the Chief. Before, as long as he was on the Alameda, he never did have to think it was anything but the Chief, like by accident. When he got flown off the ship all alone he thought That's that.

Oh, if he had only never been driven to go to the bus station. If he had not given in. If he was ever able now to shut such thoughts out of his head.

When he was still waiting to go to California, even then he did not dare ask himself why. He could not then say to himself the word Love until he was discarded by the Chief. Now he hoped he hated the man more than he loved him.

I got you into this. You were right in Honolulu, I am poison.
If you came here there is no chance. You will be lost as I am,
at least this way there is a chance.

He had let himself trust the Chief. He had surrendered on the Alameda to him and later. He had let himself believe him in Honolulu when he begged and said We can lick this together. He then went to San Diego and got back his ring. He burned all his bridges.

When Wayne got home, Mr. Burrows was there with Mama in the living room so he knew Sparky had already got to her. At first he tried to lie. He said he was damned glad Mr. Burrows was there for he was going to fight this thing to the top. They let him gas on like this for a while. Mama cried softly. Then Mr. Burrows cleared his throat.

"I would advise you, this is my opinion, to plead guilty and take your medicine. The harm is done. You cannot fight this. You will only get in deeper's all."

"Oh yes," Mama said, twisting the handkerchief in her hands. "Listen to William."

"And then," Mr. Burrows said, "you must move to another state."

Wayne sat in the chair.

"It is the only way."

Mama busted into fresh tears.

"Well I will not," Wayne said rising and standing in the middle of the room, "inflict my presence on you people any longer. I'll go tonight."

"But where?" Mama was not trying to stop him. "Please don't jump your bail!"

"To a hotel. Somewhere."

Already Wayne was thinking he had that ring upstairs to pawn and tomorrow was Friday. He thought wildly he would make the Chief take him back no matter what or now he would kill him.

But the next day who was waiting for him when he came back to his hotel from the pawn shop but Harold.

In the hallway then Harold, who always got laughed at, worked Wayne over. Harold started with the head and ended up kicking him where he lay curled up on the floor. Wayne did not cry out or try to defend himself in any way. He crawled into his hotel room and crawled up onto the bed.

Wayne went to court with Mr. Burrows and lodged his guilty plea as did all those apprehended that night. They received a fine and a good talking to. The evening newspaper didn't print any names. "Thank God," Mama said. "Oh, thank the lord." But the next day Wesley's dad came forward.

JUDGE KRAMER: Now, son, just sit down there. No, that one. This is the court stenographer, Mrs. Vesey. She is keeping a record of what we say.

WITNESS: Hi.

JUDGE KRAMER: Do you need help?

WITNESS: No.

JUDGE KRAMER: Are you comfortable?

WITNESS: I guess.

JUDGE KRAMER: How did you get down here? Did you come down in a car?

WITNESS: Uh-huh. My—we came in a car.

JUDGE KRAMER: There is nothing to be nervous about. Is there, Mrs. Vesey? Mrs. Vesey is an old hand, aren't you? Mrs. Vesey has worked in my court for almost twenty years. We do this

63

all the time. Now. Are you quite comfortable?

WITNESS: Uh-huh.

JUDGE KRAMER: Would you like a glass of water?

WITNESS: No thanks.

JUDGE KRAMER: Okay. Let me just—look—yes. Well. The
first question I have to ask you—you got
sworn in, didn't you?

WITNESS: Sorry?

JUDGE KRAMER: The bailiff swore you in on the Bible.

WITNESS: Oh, uh-huh, yes.

JUDGE KRAMER: Good. Then the first thing I have to ask you,
son, is do you know what a lie is?

WITNESS: Yes, sir, I do.

JUDGE KRAMER: You are—twelve years old.

WITNESS: Almost thirteen.

JUDGE KRAMER: Yes. Well, you are certainly old enough to
know what a lie is, aren't you?

WITNESS: I guess so.

JUDGE KRAMER: A lie is not the truth.

WITNESS: Uh-huh.

JUDGE KRAMER: Do you know what you swore on the Bible?

WITNESS: I swore I was going to tell the truth and
nothing but the truth.

JUDGE KRAMER: Very good. Now. You have an uncle.

WITNESS: Uh-huh.

JUDGE KRAMER: By the name of Wayne Smith.

WITNESS: He is one.

JUDGE KRAMER: He is one of your uncles? Yes. Do you know
your uncle—he has been brought to this
court's attention?

WITNESS: Mama said he is in trouble.

JUDGE KRAMER: Would you like to scoot over here closer,
Mrs. Vesey? Well, son, he might be and he
might not, you see.

64

WITNESS: Oh.

JUDGE KRAMER: Speak up, son.

WITNESS: I said oh.

JUDGE KRAMER: Do you know a man Wesley Gordon Senior?

WITNESS: That is Wesley's father.

JUDGE KRAMER: Yes? Now just sit back. Who is Wesley?

WITNESS: Wesley is my friend. His son. Wesley is the son. His father is Wesley Gordon too.

JUDGE KRAMER: Yes. Wesley Gordon Junior is your friend? He is your age?

WITNESS: Yes. He is in junior high. I'm not but I got held back.

JUDGE KRAMER: Yes, I see. Now.

WITNESS: I was sick.

JUDGE KRAMER: Yes. You had an accident, didn't you?

WITNESS: I got run over by a truck.

JUDGE KRAMER: I think I knew that. I was told that. You were in bed some time.

WITNESS: Uh-huh.

JUDGE KRAMER: You were confined to bed. And. This Wesley is your friend.

WITNESS: He is probably my best friend.

JUDGE KRAMER: I see. So you must spend a lot of time together.

WITNESS: I don't know if I'm his.

JUDGE KRAMER: I see. You were sick. And Wesley must have come to visit you when you were sick.

WITNESS: Yes.

JUDGE KRAMER: Did he often visit you when you were sick?

WITNESS: Sometimes.

JUDGE KRAMER: When did he visit?

WITNESS: Sometimes.

JUDGE KRAMER: Yes. Did Wesley ever spend the night with you?

65

WITNESS: I guess.

JUDGE KRAMER: Do you remember Wesley spending the night with you?

WITNESS: I think he did.

JUDGE KRAMER: I see. Do you know we have talked to Wesley? Wesley was here.

WITNESS: Here? In this room?

JUDGE KRAMER: Yes.

WITNESS: Oh.

JUDGE KRAMER: So I know Wesley, too.

WITNESS: He did spend the night with me once.

JUDGE KRAMER: You seem—do you know why you are here, son?

WITNESS: I think.

JUDGE KRAMER: Yes?

WITNESS: Wesley said something.

JUDGE KRAMER: What was that?

WITNESS: Something. I don't know.

JUDGE KRAMER: You don't?

WITNESS: I know a little.

JUDGE KRAMER: What is that?

WITNESS: Something about—I don't know.

JUDGE KRAMER: Do you love your uncle?

WITNESS: Uncle Wayne?

JUDGE KRAMER: You will have to speak up for Mrs. Vesey, son. You will have to speak loud and clear.

WITNESS: Yes, sir.

JUDGE KRAMER: You love him.

WITNESS: Yes, he is my uncle. Sure.

JUDGE KRAMER: And you love your mother.

WITNESS: Sure. Yes I do.

JUDGE KRAMER: We often want to protect those we love, don't we?

WITNESS: I suppose.

JUDGE KRAMER: Keep them safe from harm.

66

WITNESS: Yes, sir.

JUDGE KRAMER: I bet you would like everyone you love to be happy.

WITNESS: I guess.

JUDGE KRAMER: All of us feel that way. I know I do. Now, son—your friend Wesley had said—do you remember the night Wesley spent with you last fall?

WITNESS: The night.

JUDGE KRAMER: Wesley came over and spent the night with you?

WITNESS: I guess.

JUDGE KRAMER: Wesley said—you made a tent over the bed with bed sheets?

WITNESS: That night?

JUDGE KRAMER: Did you made a tent over the bed when he stayed overnight with you?

WITNESS: Yes.

JUDGE KRAMER: You told Wesley something about your Uncle that night. He says. Do you remember? Excuse me.

UNRELATED MATTER NOT TRANSCRIBED

Excuse me. I had told them not to—now—we have all the time in the world. I was asking—do you remember when Wesley was over that night—do you remember telling Wesley something about your uncle?

WITNESS: What?

JUDGE KRAMER: That's why I'm asking. That's what I'm asking. What.

WITNESS: About my Uncle Wayne?

JUDGE KRAMER: Yes.

WITNESS: I don't know.

67

JUDGE KRAMER: We are just trying to get at the bottom—the truth is very important here. I am here to find the truth. Would you like to help me find out the truth?

WITNESS: I guess. Yes.

JUDGE KRAMER: Good. Good. Well—Wesley told us you told him something about your uncle that night. Is that true?

WITNESS: I might have I guess.

JUDGE KRAMER: Your uncle was living with you?

WITNESS: Then?

JUDGE KRAMER: Yes. He was living with you, in the house with you and your sisters and your mother.

WITNESS: Both of them?

JUDGE KRAMER: Pardon?

WITNESS: Dolores is married now.

JUDGE KRAMER: I see. Yes. Getting back to Wesley.

WITNESS: Uncle Wayne lived upstairs. He slept in my room. He was at work all day.

JUDGE KRAMER: Yes. Wesley told us you told him something about your Uncle Wayne. Do you remember?

WITNESS: I guess.

JUDGE KRAMER: We are just trying to get at the truth.

WITNESS: I know.

JUDGE KRAMER: Well, did he—has your mother said anything to you about this, son?

WITNESS: About this?

JUDGE KRAMER: Has your mother said anything about what Wesley's father, for instance—did Wesley's father visit your home?

WITNESS: Yes, sir.

JUDGE KRAMER: Did he make—what did he say?

WITNESS: He said—I was not in there so long. He said. I don't feel so good.

68

JUDGE KRAMER: Have a glass—maybe you'd like that glass of water.

WITNESS: I just don't feel so good. My.

JUDGE KRAMER: I understand. Do you have to go to the bathroom?

WITNESS: No.

JUDGE KRAMER: Good. But if you want to you can go. We have all the time in the world here.

WITNESS: I know.

JUDGE KRAMER: It's a bit hot in here, isn't it?

WITNESS: Yes, sir.

JUDGE KRAMER: In my opinion, they keep these chambers overheated. Now. You were going to tell me what Wesley's father said when he visited your home.

WITNESS: Well. He said. He said Uncle Wayne was—inter—interfering with me.

JUDGE KRAMER: Interfering. Good. Wesley's father came over and he said—do you know what he meant by that?

WITNESS: I guess.

JUDGE KRAMER: Now were are getting to the—I want you to tell only the truth now. Did you tell Wesley that?

WITNESS: What?

JUDGE KRAMER: That there were certain—about this interfering.

WITNESS: Do I?

JUDGE KRAMER: Speak up, son.

WITNESS: Okay.

JUDGE KRAMER: Do you know what that means?

WITNESS: What?

JUDGE KRAMER: All right. Now son. Now I am going to—I am going to ask you directly. Did your uncle ever touch you in places—did he touch you?

WITNESS: He gave me a sponge bath.

JUDGE KRAMER: He gave you your bath? When you were sick?

WITNESS: He gave me a sponge bath. He gave me back rubs. He was nice to me.

JUDGE KRAMER: Now we're—he bathed you.

WITNESS: Yes.

JUDGE KRAMER: And when he bathed you, did he ever touch you?

WITNESS: He gave me sponge baths. I could not take real baths. I could have but we didn't know that. I could not go upstairs on my own. Anyway, they did not know if I could. The County.

JUDGE KRAMER: I see. Your uncle gave you sponge baths.

WITNESS: Yes.

JUDGE KRAMER: And when he gave you these baths, did he ever touch you down—down there?

WITNESS: There?

JUDGE KRAMER: Do you know what your genitals are, son?

WITNESS: I guess.

JUDGE KRAMER: They are—ignore Mrs. Vesey, son. She's heard everything, haven't you, Mrs. Vesey? They are your sex organs, between your legs.

WITNESS: Yes.

JUDGE KRAMER: Did your uncle ever touch you there? Just answer the question directly, son. Just answer yes or no. We only want the truth here. We are trying to get to the bottom of things. After all, I often say, if it looks as if there is black everywhere, that doesn't mean there is no white anywhere. We are trying to find the black and white truth for these purposes. We

70

want to do the right thing. So you just tell us the truth here. All right?

WITNESS: All right.

JUDGE KRAMER: Did he?

WITNESS: Touch.

JUDGE KRAMER: Did your uncle ever touch you on the genitals?

WITNESS: I think he may have.

JUDGE KRAMER: Good. That's right. That's just what we— just answer my questions.

WITNESS: Is that what inter—interfere means?

JUDGE KRAMER: Well, it can mean that, son. Yes it can.

WITNESS: Then.

1957

GRANDMA herself only owned bitty parts of her own house. The mirror next to the kitchen sink where Grandpa shaved was his alone—you would not see her fussing with her hair there. The closet in the bedroom where Grandpa's belts hung on nails was mostly his. He had his own cup and saucer and his own rocking chair—he slept in it in the evening with his head thrown back so you could see up his black nostrils. Grandma sat in the evening on the sofa like she was visiting and crocheted. She made doilies which Grandpa would not let her keep in the house so she gave them away. Even the TV belonged to Grandpa. He felt he was the only one qualified to play it.

Of course Grandpa and Grandma shared their bed. Their marriage license, covered with all kinds of fancy scrollwork, hung in a big oak frame over the headboard. They had a family Bible, too, not kept up—the pictures ended with one of Grandpa's family at the turn of the century standing straight as ramrods or sitting on kitchen chairs in front of their farmhouse. These documents were their only treasures. Oh, Grandpa sometimes picked up whatever caught his eye at auctions or won stuff at the county fair. But usually it was like when the blade part of a hoe was found to be handy to hold open the kitchen door or the crate the oil heater came in that ended up with blankets in it at the top of the stairs—most things in Grandpa's house may just as well have been washed up by the big flood. They seemed to get drawn there like it was a giant

75

magnet. I have sometimes thought that in my thirteenth year I came to Grandpa's that way too, even if Mama sent me there herself with many tears.

Something Grandma did have that was her own was a collection of salt and pepper shakers in the hutch. She had a little Mammy and an Uncle Remus, a Minny and a Mickey, bowling balls and pottery pins, cedar dice, fish leaping up out of the water, corn ears, all kinds of fruits and vegetables, silver urns made out of plastic, a devil and an angel, autumn leaves, shells and starfish, sickle moons—all the roadside junk anyone who went anywhere brought back to Grandma. But Uncle Wayne's palm trees weren't in that hutch anymore.

I knew Betty had to quit cheerleaders. I knew Dolores and Harold were not talking to us. I knew Uncle Wayne had gone somewhere for his own good.

My room upstairs next to Grandpa and Grandma's was once Uncle Wayne's but we did not talk about him now because he broke all their hearts Mama told me. So I even stopped thinking of it as his room long before you would, before I ever thought of it as mine. The windows in this room surveyed the frozen bayou and beyond that bare trees, then the railroad station and black tracks in the snow. The water tower saying WARREN NEB in red stood out painted an aluminum color against the winter sky.

Mr. Burrows brought Mama over Sundays—he was out with a vengeance to qualify to be a husband and a dad. He brought me books by the dozens. They were the Classics in shiny cardboard covers and I figured Mr. Burrows must have longed to have these books when he was an orphan. He brought me Old Rip Winkle, Natty Bumpo, Tom Sawyer and The Little Women. Many is the night I lay on the floor on my belly while Grandpa snored and read Mr. Burrows's books. When I finally broke down and asked him for more he smiled showing his dog teeth. You could hear him patting himself on the back. He said

A mighty frigate is a book.

Mr. Burrows was also fond of saying to me

The child is the father of the man.

This was the price I had to pay. In spite of Mr. Burrows, though, I liked the stories and the children in them.

Mama said she missed me, she missed me. She fussed over me every Sunday. She fussed setting the table and drove Grandma crazy in the kitchen until she said Janice get out of here so I can make the gravy. Mama watched me eat like a hawk.

One Sunday when Mr. Burrows was helping her put on her coat I heard Mama whisper "Dad looks so bad."

So I started looking at Grandpa and she was right. Grandpa was caving in on himself. His chest was like that sink-hole downtown that opened up with no warning whatsoever one day and started gobbling up parking meters and cars. Grandpa's cheeks got hollow and his red face, covered with broke veins, was now pasty.

It snowed all winter that winter without a break. Snow was cast up by the bushel by the plows along the Main Street. Old snow was always turning brown in the ruts of snow and sand only briefly to be replaced by clean white snow before this cycle continued. The winter world was quiet. I didn't mind. The floorboards were cold as icecubes. Frost grew thick inside the window panes. The blizzards whipped in across the plains without letup and in on the tail end of one came Dad.

DAD watched me for three whole days but I didn't know. I may have seen him but no one would have guessed. For it was like Dad was dead and then all of a sudden Dad was back but he was changed. He had lost all his pretty red hair. He was not a smiler anymore. He did not need people.

Dad told me he stood in the snow across from Warren Elementary and tears ran down his face when he saw me come down the steps, so careful, with all the other children running out into the snow. Dad said I was with one exception the spitting image of himself.

On the third day Dad put me in his car. I was too scared to cry out. He did not drive away immediately. He slid me across the seat and got in and sat there looking at me. I knew then it was Dad.

I was scared but also amazed—this was really Dad with me in the car. As he spoke I memorized his dashboard. When I looked down at the seat covers, I saw they were woven out of straw where they were not plastic. The seat felt warm under my hand. Dad's heater put out gusts of hot air. The windshield was fogged up. Dad spoke softly. He lit a cigarette. He took off my stocking cap and ruffled my hair with his hand.

"What did you learn in school today?"

I didn't answer any of his questions.

"I said what did you learn in school?"

Then he put out his cigarette and put the car into gear. He wiped the inside of the window with a chamois. The water streamed down. He pulled away from the curb.

"I would like something to eat now. Wouldn't you? How about a burger?"

I didn't say anything.

"You know, where I'm staying they have great burgers. They fry the bun on the grill and they put on sweet pickle relish. You can have relish and onions and lots of ketchup if you want. How would you like a shake? Would you like a chocolate shake?"

There was nothing to see on my side but fogged window. I could not jump out of that car. I could not wave to anyone.

"Did you know that when I was a boy I worked as a soda jerk? Do you know what that is? Sundaes and shakes, I could make whatever the customer wanted. They have all sorts of fountain treats at the place next door to where I'm staying."

Good-bye old Court House. Good-bye old Sears. Good-bye old Piggly-Wiggly.

"Maybe you want a cup of black coffee instead?" Dad teased. "You don't drink coffee? I thought maybe you drink coffee and smoke already. You are so big now, aren't you? You're almost, you know, you're thirteen now, aren't you?"

Good-bye Grandpa and Grandma. Good-bye. And I have never yet had a cake with a sugar HAPPY BIRTHDAY on it and cowboys and now I am too old.

Dad sighed and stopped talking. We were at the highway. It was getting darker. Grandma wouldn't even wonder yet. Grandma wouldn't think He has fell down. Not yet. Grandpa was not even home from work. Not yet. The lights were not on in the kitchen. Grandma was not yet banging pans on the burners. The big mixing bowl was still sitting up on the shelf.

"This is it." Dad switched off the car and turned to me. "What'll it be? You want that burger? Or maybe you would like to have a grilled cheese instead. What'll it be?"

I didn't answer. I looked at the silver button with the keyhole

79

on the glove compartment. I remembered Wesley's mama's canary. Dad's car said

on the dash.

"Got to eat something. Ain't you hungry?"

Finally I shook my head no.

"Better eat. We have a long trip ahead of us."

I looked at Dad hard. He had his arm thrown up along the steering wheel and his head cocked to one side.

"Don't be afraid," he said. "I am your Dad, ain't I?"

I didn't ask Where you taking us? I just thought Go along with it and get away.

"That's better. You aren't scared, are you? That's good. It's so good to see you. I missed you so. You may not believe it. That's okay. You don't have to. I have waited so long. You will see how much I love you. It's tore me apart not having you kids. So what'll it be? A burger? You can have anything you want. Sky's the limit. I mean it."

I ducked my head and put my hand on the door handle. It was cold.

"No no." Dad reached over and lifted my hand off the handle. "Sorry no."

The wind was billowing, dipping, sliding around the car. Old snow was blowing up against the windshield now, forming a scallopy frame for the dark outside.

"You're going to have to stay put in the car, understand?"

W HEN I opened the door snow blew in. Icy bits stuck on my face. Drifts were now losing their tops. I looked around and I wanted to cry for I had got up all my courage and I was nowhere. The car was somewhere off the highway away from all the lights in the middle of nowhere.

Dad is smart.

When he came back I was sitting where he left me, good as gold. I heard the trunk open and something clunk in. Then Dad came to the driver's side and got in the car. He handed me back my limb. The metal parts were freezing cold from being in the trunk. When I had put my limb back on and pulled on my pants, Dad took our dinner out of a paper bag. He gave me a burger.

"She said How do you want it? and I said The works."

I took a bite. Dad opened a cardboard container, stripped the cover off a straw, plunged it into the shake. He set the shake down on the car seat beside me.

"How's yours?" Dad was chewing his like a condemned man. "Mine's good. Boy! I didn't eat all day. I was too keyed up. I knew today was the day. Hell of a note when a man has to sneak around town after his own boy." Dad was taking me into his confidence. He was trying to apologize. "Hell of a note. How's that burger?"

I looked away, supposing you could even see out the window.

Dad chawed some more then he took the lid off his coffee.

"Look at that out there. That's all right. I got a good long nap."

I wanted to ask Which way we going? I thought if we drove through Lincoln I could get away. But I didn't know where Lincoln was anymore.

Dad smacked his lips and gobbled up his burger. I could only eat a bite of mine. I felt sick. But I tried to say It is okay. I was a teenager now. A phrase they used to use all the time in physical therapy floated up in my brain

THE WILL POWER TO SUCCEED

I had learned to walk. All around me old people could not. Some of them lost both their legs. Some of them could never learn again.

Grandpa would come in and say Where is my dinner? Grandma would be on the phone. Grandpa would grab the phone away from her.

"You are scared, aren't you? I don't blame you. Believe me, son, if there was any other way, I would of done it. Can't be helped." Dad's coffee was steaming up in his face. "I feel like hell about this, believe you me. Would you like a little music?"

So Dad switched on the radio. The lights behind the stations pulsed a little. I thought Maybe the battery will run down. Dad pushed the chrome buttons on the radio and turned the dial until he found what he wanted.

"Do you watch Hit Parade? I don't know what you like anymore, do I? But you don't know much about me either. What you know is pretty bad, huh? I was in pretty bad shape back then, wasn't I? You remember? You know what my problem was? I bet your mama told you I was a drunk. Well, I was. I'm not now. Not anymore. I'm a new man, Son. You'll see."

Dad wiped his mouth with a paper napkin.

"You haven't even put a dent in that shake. What's wrong? Too cold? That's all right. Here, give me that. Let's wrap that up. Maybe you'll want to finish it on the road. We have a long drive ahead of us."

Dad wrapped up my burger in waxed paper and put it back in the bag. He held up the shake with the straw pointing at me but I shook my head.

"Boy, cat's sure got your tongue tonight, hasn't he?"

Dad put the cover back on the shake and set it in the little groove between the seats.

He smiled at me.

You felt sorry for Dad. I was confused, too, as to whether it was kidnapping when it was your own kid.

Dad reached over and felt my cheek with the back of his hand. He caught the tear that fell from my eye. He bent over the bag and the rest of the junk on the car seat. He put his arms around me.

My face pressed into Dad's jacket. It was wool and some little drops still clung to it from the snow. His embrace was not the way it used to be when he squeezed you to death.

DAD was fearless. He drove right into that blizzard. At the very first the snow only came down like confetti. In the car lights the highway was like a tunnel in the storm. If you looked hard you could see lights on in the windows in the farm houses closest to the road.

They were already going to bed there—the dog was out branding a drift. These houses were half buried in the snow, with a patch shoveled out in front of the door and a path to the barn. On each roof of these houses there is always a place like a finger smudge where the snow melts at the base of the chimney. On the side of them in the snow there are icicles hanging under the stove pipe.

Dad's radio said it was going to be a doozy, then it faded out into static. Dad flicked it off.

Under the tire chains the sand and snow made a sound like teeth grinding.

Dad lit a cigarette and cracked the window. Icy wind swirled in and circled my neck and my wrists.

Dad talked to keep his spirits up. He told me about his church and the basic precepts of his faith. He told me about how God had decided not to take him at the last minute. He told me the Pope had a mess of brats running wild in the basement of the Vatican.

The storm got deeper. Cars passed us going the other way. The brown tire tracks in front of Dad's car narrowed then we were alone on the highway.

Dad sang in the car. He sang Blue Skies Smiling at Me, April Showers, Stormy Weather, Get Your Coat and Hat, Singin in the Rain, It's a Lovely Day Today, The Continental. He asked me if I liked to sing.

"We used to sing all the time, remember? We used to sing coming back from your Grandpa's in the car. Remember?"

Dad's red hair had a part in it then like the edge of a ruler.

"Regular sing-alongs."

The storm hung like a gray curtain before us. Dad sang The Autumn Leaves, Moonlight in Vermont, April in Paris, I Like New York in June, Don't Sit Under the Apple Tree, I'm Dreaming of a White Christmas.

No more Christmas.

Dad said the first Christmas he spent away from us he lived in a rented room in someone's house and for Christmas Eve supper he ate a turkey sandwich with mayo and drank a whole fifth bottle of Jim Beam. That was before God decided to give him a second chance.

"Don'tcha wanna to pick one now? What songs do you know from your school? Do you know Shortnin Bread? I bet you know that one.

Two little chillun
Layin in bed
One of them sick
De other half dead
Call for de doctor
Doctor said
Feed them chillun on shortnin bread

Dad sang in his sweet tenor voice.

"Sing along! Don't be shy!"

Dad sang all the verses. The tires were getting slithery even under Dad's chains. The tire tracks were now more like pencil lines. Dad beat the wheel in time with his singing.

Soon he was not singing anymore and just beating. "Gene Krupa. There's a great drummer. You know, I'm getting awful tired of hearing myself talk. I may not ever talk again. What would you think of that? I may never open up my mouth. Course, I would have to open my mouth to eat, wouldn't I? Or I would starve. Or they would have to feed me through the gut. In Paris they like goose livers. Did you know that? They're crazy about goose livers. And because they are so crazy about them they go to great lengths to fatten up those old geese over there. The geese, their whole life is nothing but a banquet. They put a tube down their gullets and shove the food in, stuff those birds, stuff them till they're ready to bust. Seriously, though, I'm getting awful tired of hearing myself talk. Why don'tcha say just one thing? Just one. You have not even said you're glad to see me. I hope you aren't too mad at me. You mad at me?" Dad reached over in front of me and pushed the button on the glove compartment.

His hand came out not with a gun or a knife but with a Hershey bar. "If you," Dad said, holding the bar in the flat of his hand and steering with the other. "If you say just one thing I'll give you this Hershey bar. It has nuts in it." He tipped up the bar so I could read the wrapper. "Just one thing."

85

I always liked chocolate. I looked at the brown and silver candy bar in front of me.

"What do you say?"

I reached out for it. Dad snatched it away.

"Oh, no!" Dad laughed delightedly. "First say it."

I asked, "Where we going?"

Dad didn't say anything. He dropped the candy bar into my lap. I peeled the wrapper off the chocolate. I said to myself I wonder if they ever get the bars mixed up? What if No Nuts came in the Nuts wrapper? What if all over America people would have to learn to ask for No Nuts permanent when they really wanted some? The chocolate melted down over my teeth.

"Can't I have some?"

I broke off a chunk and put it in Dad's hand. He popped it into his mouth.

"I would of," he said, "give it to you anyway, had you not even talked."

D AD stopped for gas and got out to pay. The snow around us was now like a cyclone and the station was the eye. I had to go bad but I held it. I could see Dad in the office talking to the man. Dad came out with Cokes. He offered me one but I shook my head no. We pulled out into the storm.

We were the only ones on the road in the whole U.S. Dad's headlights were the only white in all that black.

Dad told me about the pioneers who traveled across this same prairie in their covered wagons, how people died from thirst and heat stroke and the animals staggered in their traces, how over the mountains they went. They crossed the desert for many months, they passed the bleached bones of cattle and horses, bones picked clean by the vultures.

"And they reached the land of milk and honey and they made the desert bloom. The good Lord sent the bees to eat up all the locusts, they stung them to death first. People went around thrusting their bare hands into the warm brown earth and it was good, they liked most in those days to walk around with bare feet in the scented evening. They invented the steam engine and the McCormick reaper. John Deere dipped in his oar. Irrigation was invented. It must have been sort of a shame when the electric light came."

Then Dad shut up. When I woke there were only two little peep holes on the windshield over the heater to see through. Dad said "Damnit, gonna have to stop."

So even Dad gave up. Somewhere in Nebraska or Colorado he pulled into a cabin court and went into the office.

All the cabins sat in a half circle in the night. All their windows were dark but for the office at the end, and then as I watched the neon sign went out for good.

Dad came out and moved the car. He picked me up and walked with long steps through the snow to our cabin. He had to sweep the snow off the doorstep with his foot. He had to sweep it away from in between the screen door and the door where it was piled up like the sand in Wesley's ant farm.

Inside, Dad turned on the electric heater. I sat on the bed watching him as he brought in his suitcase and checked the windows. He let down the blinds, turned on the light in the bathroom. He went in and peered into the toilet. He came out of the bathroom looking pleased. He said it was cozy as could be. Life of Riley, Dad said.

There were print curtains at the window with cactus on them. There was an easy chair in the corner and a dresser on one wall. Dad turned out the overhead light and switched on the lamp beside the bed. He asked me if I wanted to pee so I went in and peed.

The door had a hook and eye on it, Dad could pull that off easy. The little window was set high in the wall. I could not climb out to freedom.

Mr. Burrows would be comforting Mama. Betty would ask if they could have hot cocoa. Poor Mama. Police cars in front of our house again.

"Hey, give the other fella a chance, huh?"

I came out of the bathroom. Dad went in and left the door open a crack. I took off my coat. All the heat in the room came out of a heater in the wall but stopped three inches from it so you had to hold your fingers out to feel it.

"Isn't much good, is it?"

Dad came out zipping up his pants. He pulled back the coverlet on the bed and patted one of the pillows. He tested the mattress then he straightened up and pulled out his shirt tails.

"Better get undressed. Soon as this passes, I want to be back on the road. Son," Dad said sitting on the edge of the bed and pulling me over in front of him. "This is the only way."

I gazed into his blue eyes.

"The only way," Dad said sadly. Then he let me go. He stood up and opened his suitcase on the floor. He handed me his p.j. top.

So I went around to the other side of the bed and sat down. I took off my shirt and T-shirt. I unlaced my shoe and dropped it on the floor. Behind me Dad was whistling through his teeth. I wriggled out of my pants and unstrapped my leg. I could feel Dad watching me. I left the sock on my stump.

"I'll take that."

Dad turned the leg over and over, examining it in the weak light. Then he went to the closet and put it up on the top shelf.

I put on Dad's top. The sleeves hung down. He was standing there watching me then he came over and lifted up the bed-clothes. I slid in.

Dad picked up one of the pillows and took a blanket and sat down in the chair and took off his shoes. The lamp shade on the table beside me jiggled as Dad burrowed into his chair. He pulled the blanket up over himself.

"Go asleep now."

I closed my eyes.

MAYBE I snoozed. Behind my eyelids it was yellow—the color of the walls in the physical therapy room.

I looked at that room. The little steps up and down. The ramp. The strip of carpet. Rings. Medicine balls resting on the floor. I could not look at that room with the people in it.

The wall full of windows. Outside the balcony with the brown firs dying in their tubs.

Weights hanging. Charts of MUSCLE GROUPS. Gray desk in the corner with clipboards—there were lollypops hid in the drawer of that desk. Calendars and crayola drawings. Sticks and canes, crutches and limbs to show you.

One more chin-up, up, no hands, no one will pick you up this time, not this time, you know how, you can cry all you want, can't he?

So I looked at the little cabins in the snow around the flagpole and I counted the ordinary steps there would be between them. I saw the rock-edged paths where the bald earth was maybe blown clean, measured the drifts of snow. I saw myself dead on my belly froze stiff.

Oh, my gosh! There seems to be someone.

I looked over between my lashes at Dad sleeping in his chair.

His chin was on his chest. He had his arms under the blanket. Next to him the electric heater burned red like it was painted on the wall. Dad's head rose in tiny jerks along with his chest.

I trusted my arms even though one was broke twice. I trusted my weight, which was slight. There was not much I could do but I could do what I could and I knew what that was.

The resourceful boy swung out of bed.

One toe was on the floor. Oh, it was really a tiny cabin after all, not nearly so big without Dad moving through it. I let myself fall through the air and like a spider caught the wall.

I looked back. Dad was sleeping like a baby snuggly-wuggly under his blanket.

The air smelled like dust. I inched to the door. The knob was not so cold as you expected though the wall on my other hand was. I turned that key.

Terry slithers like a snake through the long savannah grasses.

I cracked open the door and slipped through.

I pulled the door shut behind me, screen door creaking open from my weight, a warm puff following me out, then I was out, out in the blizzard flat on my back.

The snow drift pillowed me there. The blizzard was howling. I lay still for a minute. I half expected the door to open and Dad to say What's up?

You could sleep right here.

Oh, my gosh! There seems to be someone froze in this glacier from centuries before!

I sat up and maybe I screamed a little. I looked down the crescent of cabins, the longest line in the deepest snow, so long I couldn't see the last cabin where the neon sign was dead anyway. Ice hit my teeth.

So I started crawling. No use trying to hop and hold the cabin walls. I crawled as fast as I could. My knee hit something and it hurt.

The wind whistled Dixie in my ears. The wind blew so hard nothing stuck. I had to close my eyes to crawl. I crawled and crawled.

Then I was being yanked up out of the snow. Dad was jerking me up and throwing me down. Dad jerked me up and into a wall I heard a crack like the siding on the cabin. Dad closed in on me, he fell on me, staggered, swooped me up, dragged me in his arms.

He pulled me inside our cabin and shook me and shook me I was screaming and the arm was flopping around at my side I screamed and screamed.

Dad's eyebrows were full of snow and snow was on his eyelashes snow like confetti was at the corners of his mouth and his shoulders were covered with it his teeth were clicking.

"Little bastard little shit!"

Dad pushed me onto the bed and pulled the covers off under me and pushed me against my chest and yelled I realized my arm was broke again Dad broke it against the side of the cabin.

"Dad Dad Dad!"

He ran to the suitcase and took out his rope I tried to tell him but he only yelled at me he pushed me down and pushed me down Dad tied me down.

91

WHAT do you want me to do?" Dad asked.

He was not talking to me.

I licked the snot off my lip. My arm did not hurt. Maybe I could not feel pain anymore.

Dad was praying in the dark and the dim light coming from the heater. He had both his hands clasped together. He was on his knees at the side of the bed. He had been talking to God for a long time. He would not listen to me.

Every once in a while he would get up and check the knots. I lay stone still. Then Dad would get back on his knees.

He had fetched a can of gas from the car, one of those red safety cans with the wire handle. He had set it there next to the bathroom door.

Dad continued to pray.

"Has not this man-child suffered enough for his transgressions? Must this young green life be taken? Must you suffer this little child to come to you?"

Dad prayed until dawn and beyond. Whenever the real dawn was it was pearly between the slats of the blinds when Dad finished praying and got up. God had not answered him yet.

He fell into the chair.

I had slept through most of this only waking every time I again thought Dad had set us on fire. Now by raising my head I could see Dad sitting with blank eyes.

I asked for a glass of water but Dad would not listen—his ear was trained only on God.

He sat there a long time. It was quiet outside. The blizzard was gone.

Then Dad stirred. He sat up with his elbows on his knees and regarded me with sorrow.

"Do you know what I was going to give you?" he said quietly. "I was going to give you a horse of your own. Really. All your very own. There's plenty of land for a horse where my new house is to be. There's plenty of boys who would like a horse. There's plenty of boys who would jump at the chance to have a horse with a saddle with their own initials burned into it. Maybe you just aren't old enough to accept the responsibility of such a gift. Maybe you are just not mature enough."

Dad went to the bathroom and pissed. He came back and sat down. He said "You should just see where we were going to live." And then he told me all about his new house.

"Are you going to burn us up, Dad?"

"What?"

"Are you going to set us on fire?" I croaked out.

He wagged his hand, maybe maybe not.

"Or just me?" I asked.

Dad hung his head.

Then all of a sudden Dad brightened up.

"What kind of car you want?" he asked rubbing his hands together. "Now don't answer right off the bat. Think about it."

I could not follow.

"Anything but a sport car," he amended.

Dad paced around and didn't hear my answer. He sat down in his chair again. "Oh, God."

I thought he was going to talk to God again but he said no more for a minute then, "I wanted you so bad," Dad groaned.

He was close to tears. He was more like the old Dad then.

Through his fingers he said "When you were born I was so happy, even if I was in the service and missed it. I loved you already in your pictures. I was so glad to have a boy. And I have

93

made so many plans over these past months. Wouldn't you like a basketball net on the front of the garage?" Dad was begging me to want it. "I have dreamed of hearing a basketball out on the driveway. I would look up from my paper and see you. I would like a boy who worships God and tries to change things for the better because God knows I have not been able to though I have struggled prodigiously. I just want my boy."

I started crying for Dad. Hot tears swam in my eyes. Snot blocked up my throat. I started crying and I cried until I lost my breath and had to stop so I would not drown.

"I know," Dad said from the corner. "You love your dad, don't you?"

"Yes I do!" I shouted like I was in a revival meeting.

"You see how much I love you?"

I dropped my head back on the bed and gazed at the ceiling.

"Dad, I will never be," I said.

"Oh, Lord God."

I was scared Dad was going back in his trance again but I had to say the truth. I didn't want to lie even to him anymore.

"Dad, I will never be. I can't. I will never be a real boy like you want."

"Oh Lord God Jesus you poor boy."

"I can't be now."

"What did he do to you?"

I thought he meant God, but he meant Uncle Wayne.

S OMEWHERE around noon, God told Dad to go to Denver so he woke me up and untied me.

Dad was at first upset that he might have cut off circulation. He felt terrible when he found out he broke my arm.

94

And that's how I learned Dad was once a Scout himself. He busted up a dresser drawer and devised a splint.

It was blazing white sunlight when we set out from the cabin court to continue our journey across the plains. The snow plows had been over the road though not down to the blacktop. Dad's chains clinked on the asphalt.

Dad was cheerful in that white day. He seemed to have had his purpose renewed. He whistled a happy tune.

"I think we ought to find some local cafe where we can get a mess of bacon and eggs and maybe even pancakes. How's that strike you?"

I thought Maybe I can get away from Dad before he changes his mind and kills me after all.

"Wheatcakes!" Dad snapped. "With maple syrup dripping down them all over the plate."

"Sounds good!"

"When we get to Denver," he said, suddenly real sober. "I want to call your mama. No, I mean it, put an end to the awful suspense as to where you are. As long as we're safe in Denver, why not call her? Would you like to have a word with her?"

"Sure," I said. "That would be great."

"Poor Janice."

That was all he said. He'd already told me in the night she was an unfit mother and should be torn apart limb by limb and scattered all over Canaan for what she let Uncle Wayne do to me. When I said Uncle Wayne didn't do anything to me, Dad got furious and screamed how he read all about the sex ring of young boys.

"Mama must be worried sick," I said.

"Serves her right but we'll call her anyway, give her a how-dee!" Dad said like Grand Ol Opry. "Only you can't let on where we have gone, understand?"

"Oh yes."

"Good because we are on a weekend pass with the Lord as it is."

So we drove across the white plains on that road straight as an arrow to Denver and I kept Dad in a good humor. He either forgot about eating or had thought better of stopping, so I ended up chewing on that burger from last night.

Dad told knock-knock jokes and sang more songs. He asked me riddles. I was delirious. The pain from my arm was always about to black me out. So I started thinking Dad was the best pal a boy ever had.

Dad promised me that day he would buy me all sorts of things. He would buy me an erector set plus a set of Lincoln Logs. I could have Monopoly and Chinese Checkers. He was going to build me a tree house on a telephone-type pole because we didn't have any trees in our yard yet and put a phone in it hooked up to the kitchen so I would not be late for dinner. I could have my own deer rifle for we would often go hunting together on the Western Slope. Dad asked me if I ever had a red wagon though he should have known I never, so he said I could have a red one or any other color in the world. He said he planned on entering me in the soap-box derby but he warned me he couldn't help—dads could not build your car for you. "Sorry, Son, there you're on your own."

"I forgot the Teddy bear," I said.

Dad said You bet, and a little pail and shovel for the beach. I asked Dad for everything I could think of. By the time we reached Denver I had more toys than Wesley.

I got so carried away I forgot everything I'd said to Dad in the cabin court. It had not sunk in anyway. It had all gone right in one ear and out the other. Dad still thought I was the boy he wanted.

I was raving by the time Dad drove up in front of his rented house in Denver that night. They said I was talking in tongues. My eyes were sunk deep in my face and I had pissed all over myself. Dad wasn't in much better shape. He didn't even recognize his own twin when he saw Uncle Bill open the front door.

1969

WHEN Grandma died Uncle Walter got Grandpa's gun although Grandpa once promised it to me. Aunt Eileen got the Bible. Mama ended up with the rocking chair. Dolores and Betty picked over Grandma's little store of costume jewelry. Aunt Mona didn't take anything.

"Mona, you got to want something for goodness sake!"

"Yes, for goodness sake. Oh, Lord! Remember this hat?"

Mama and Eileen acted like it was their birthday party.

I could see Aunt Mona might have liked to have some old photos, for her hand hovered briefly before Eileen swept them up like you do so many playing cards to make a hand.

I too thought it would be nice to have something out of that house. But the last day, when it sat ready for the salvage and I could take anything left I wanted, I didn't. When I finally did leave that house for good, I only took some old blankets from upstairs and threw them in the back of my van.

I had one suitcase full of clothes, a box of LPs and my stereo, some other junk. But truly, when I moved out, it was just like I'd been a boarder.

Grandma was buried next to Grandpa the weekend before Memorial Day. Some of the graves in the graveyard were already decorated with flags and flowers. Mama read the familiar stones out loud while we walked.

"And that's your Aunt Lola who died from the flu when I was just tiny."

When we reached the graveside, I saw that only Grandpa's

name, of course, was yet on their stone, and as far as I know it still may be as I have never gone back.

While the preacher talked the girls cried. Mama, Aunt Eileen and Uncle Walter cried. The people from Grandma's church cried. I did not. Aunt Mona, too, stood dry-eyed—no one knew what she was thinking those whole four days.

In the car, Mama sat back and lit a filtertip and said to Mr. Burrows: "The last part of my dad is gone now."

It was funny but I was probably the only one who knew the real Grandma anymore, because I lived with her—this little lady everyone knew was going to fall clean apart when Grandpa died. She did not.

WHY do you know she never even learned how to buy herself a dress without him along."

In reality, Grandma loved the intricacies of her checking account at the bank. She traveled on her lifetime pass from the railroad to visit her children and remaining relatives. She told me she would fly if she had to.

She had her pension from the railroad and she supplemented this by raising strawberries and beans in the plot out back. She canned tomatoes and put up jelly—Grandma had the feel for jelly. She went regular to church Circle. She had continued her crochet work—Grandma's dolls that sat on pillows in the bedroom were coveted. She heard of this man in Mohawk who made lamps with the shade matching the doll's dress and she wrote him a letter. From then on, Grandma had her daily quota of crochet.

Grandma took in boarders—she always had a man from the factory in the basement of our house. Most of these men were solitary souls. It didn't take a genius to see that not a single one came from anywhere or was on his way to anywhere. Then he would be gone and there'd be another one on the front porch with a scrap of paper in his hand. Then when I was fifteen Bud came and he stayed.

Like Mr. Burrows, Bud was an orphan but he lived with relations in Freemont until the last of them died and then he moved to Warren, so it was like out of one house and into the other. Bud was a mouth breather, which is to say he was not very bright and meeting him you knew he would never rise above janitor. But right from the beginning Bud was Grandma's boy. Even if her children did not approve, on Saturdays Bud drove her downtown in Grandpa's Studebaker.

Bud was a workhorse and this endeared him to Grandma for once she got that house in her hands she seemed intent on making it a showplace. Grandma was a hard task-master. Oh, she never raised her voice—all she had to do was look like she was dying of mental cruelty. And by and by, through these means, Grandma got done everything Grandpa never. She finished what Grandpa barely contemplated. She straightened what Grandpa was happy to leave crooked. She patched up what Grandpa had himself spurned. So when they sold that old shack, it brought seven-thousand dollars.

One summer I helped Bud paint that house. Grandma sent us back to Sears to get just the right shade of sky blue for the porch ceiling. She had us strip the trellises of any leftover morning-glory vines. She saw to it that we did not omit anything. Grandma made us take a razor-blade to the window panes so not one single fleck of paint was left on the glass. Grandma didn't miss a trick.

Endlessly Grandma sang the praises of Bud to any neighbor lady that would listen. But Bud wasn't all Grandma thought he was. I learned that the summer I painted the house alongside him. For one thing, Bud was no stranger to sex and out of earshot of Grandma he would boast of his exploits. Now I can just see Bud red to the roots of his hair at the door of the whorehouse. But then I was a total innocent who all through high school never even had the courage to ask a girl for a date and I egged Bud on whilst we painted screens propped up against stepladders in the shade of the garage. What is it like, what does it feel like? I would ask him, and he'd say It depends, sometimes like the softest feather pillow but wet and sometimes like it has teeth liable to bite your whang off. To hear Bud tell it, those whores like to scratch each other's eyes out over him because he had the biggest one in the state of Nebraska and you know what it takes to satisfy that kind of woman. Bud was supposedly a professional Peeping Tom too, forever hopping over hedges and evading bloodthirsty dogs.

"Some night you're gonna get caught," I warned him.

"Guess I'm just a pussy slave," he snickered in reply, and for months after that, every time Bud as much as hissed that word or even just mouthed it across the dinner table, we'd fall into histronics together.

All those years Grandma fed Bud and me three square meals but she never sat down and ate with us—she liked standing up at the sink and picking off her plate. In the morning Grandma fed us biscuits and fried eggs, which she speeded up by spooning hot grease over, or oatmeal with a blob of brown sugar melting in the middle. At noon I found in my lunch bucket bologna or American cheese or deviled ham. At night it was hamburgers and coleslaw, or fried chicken and Minute rice, tuna and noodle, or macaroni and cheese.

By and by I noticed that if there was a bigger pork chop it somehow ended up on Bud's plate, or juicier marrow bone or fatter chicken thigh or the potato with the unburned skin. With self-pity, this adolescent felt many times the real orphan. Maybe Grandma didn't have that much love to waste. Maybe when Grandpa was alive Grandma couldn't see beyond him—he was like a Mount Everest with a million tons of snow on it ready to come thundering down on top of you. So when

Grandpa died, Grandma seemed to wake and survey the land-
scape and saw to her vast relief she didn't have to do for another
again, so she did the bare minimum for me. Maybe it was easier
to love Bud. My own mama could not often tear herself away
from Lincoln anymore and when she did visit always said My
you are shooting up just like a weed, long after I stopped
growing altogether and went into the factory myself.

And so my teenage years passed and beyond.

Bud was not very bright but he was not a total fool. When
Grandma died he did not stick around. He knew he was not
welcome. He packed his suitcase and was gone with no good-
bye. He did not even attend her funeral.

I cried for Grandma. After we buried her when everyone was
sitting around her living room gassing while waiting for the
church ladies to put dinner on the table, when I was at last safe
up in my own room under that old Map of the World, I put my
face on the bed and cried long and hard into the chenille spread.

"Better blow your nose now."

Aunt Mona was pushing a handkerchief at me. I took it and
blew.

"Get it out of your system?"

I folded the handkerchief and blew again. I tried to give it
back but she waved it away like it was now ruined forever.

"They have laid on a beautiful spread down there. Aren't you
going to eat some?"

"I guess."

"Baked beans. I think I saw meatloaf. You like meatloaf,
don't you?"

"Yeah."

But we did not stir. Mona walked to my window and gazed
out over the tops of the trees' branches.

"What will you do now?" she said after a while.

"Everyone's been asking me that."

"Well?" Her face had a kind look on it.

"Uncle Sparky says I should move into Lincoln and start at Chicks."

Mona smiled. "And would that suit you?"

"I like Warren. But."

"But what?"

"Well," I said, "I can't think why anyone would want to stay on at the factory. But on the other hand, if you didn't live in Warren, why would you want to live in Lincoln?"

"I'm sure your mama would be happy to have you in Lincoln."

To this I just smirked.

"I'm sure she would be happy to have you closer," Mona said, but I could tell she didn't believe that either.

"Now what about that future, Craig?" was how Mr. Burrows put it. "Not too late for the Junior College, you know." Mr. Burrows had not yet given up on my higher education.

He had moved Mama to the suburbs. Theirs was a two-bedroom tract house and one of the bedrooms they had made into this den with a rolltop desk with a pipe-rack full of pipes Mr. Burrows rotated like tires. Mr. Burrows would lay in there reading in his recliner that had magic fingers just like a motel bed. From this position on Sundays he was always reminding me that the door was open for fatherly chats.

No one, however, had insisted Why don't you move right in, they loved me so much—they were not encouraging any more kids to come stay with them now that they had Dolores all married off again.

I never had asked for anything and when I first brought up the van, Mr. Burrows must have been afraid I was going to turn into a hippie, for he began to quiz me. "Are you going to open up a florist shop?" he asked, smiling like Richard Nixon.

"No, I have saved some money and I want to take a trip but I need a little help."

104

"Oh, see the U.S.A.," he said joking.

"Maybe."

"Maybe." His eyes narrowed. "A van. I have never ridden in one. Does this mean perhaps you plan to circumnavigate the globe in same?" Mr. Burrows knit all his fingers together and looked at me over the tops of his knuckles.

"Maybe I'll go visit one of those national parks you're always recommending and torment the bears."

"Sarcasm is a poor substitute for wit, Craig."

"Lots of my classmates are in the war already."

Mr. Burrows turned suddenly grave and nodded like he understood how I hated so not getting to lose my other leg.

Mr. Burrows himself who was turned down by the army must have wanted once to run away from his orphanage to the circus or something, for at length to my surprise he wrote out a check. Of course he had me sign a piece of paper to the effect that all my chattels would revert to him. Then he begged me not to buy a German product.

I didn't have a home. I didn't have a girl. There wasn't anything holding me there. I figured my life thus far hadn't amounted to a hill of beans. Now was the time. And as for the loan from Mr. Burrows that I never meant to pay back in the first place—the way I looked at it he could take it out of that ten-thousand-five-hundred dollars that I never saw for my leg.

I had been on family vacations as a child. I had been on a bus to Omaha. I had been on the train to Kansas. I had flown a plane to Arkansas to see the McMullens for my high school graduation present. But I had never gone anywhere under my own steam.

Now I drove like a bat out of hell. I drove straight through sleeping by the side of the road. I drove like it was my job to—I thought along the way I'd be a good truck driver pulling down lots of money and living the life of the road if I wanted to.

I didn't stop for the Snake Farm or the Mormon Tabernacle or Caves Next Exit. I skipped the sights. I didn't browse for any souvenirs I knew would be junk anyway. It would drive you crazy anyway if you tried to pick out some one thing for everyone you ever loved. And when I came back from Arkansas that time with gifts they treated them like poison the way they always treated me after Uncle Wayne.

I crossed the plains. I crossed the Continental Divide. I crossed the desert. I followed that pioneer trail Dad was not able to trace to its conclusion.

I thought often of that long ago trip with Dad and at night in my van sleeping at the side of the road I dreamed of Dad as I had each night since. Dad always came to me in these dreams with half a head—in answer, you felt, to Wesley's and my childhood question of how much of you would be left. So when Dad tried to talk to me in these dreams I couldn't understand, since naturally, blood would be bubbling up in Dad's mouth, because, after the police took me away and Uncle Bill left Dad alone in his rented house he blew his brains out with a shotgun down in the basement. Frustrated, Dad would wave his arms semaphore style in these dreams.

I often thought too, on my journey, of Aunt Mona and Uncle Arthur, two people who I never got a chance to know because of what Mr. Burrows would term Time and Tide. I had never met my Uncle Arthur and my aunt only at two funerals. Up in my room after we buried Grandma, Mona described their move to California in the Depression: how Grandpa had called this a fool's errand, how everything they owned in the world was in the rumble-seat or lashed to the top of the car, how the radiator kept boiling over, how they kipped out under the stars, how joyful they felt when they reached balmy Los Angeles where grapefruit grew on the trees.

I drove straight through. I did not stop. It was night when I pulled up in front of that house.

I turned off the ignition. I sat back in my seat.

The house was hacienda-style. It was painted white. The roof was tile and so were the window sills.

My van creaked cooling down. I sat there. All sorts of things ran through my head. Presently the porch light went out but I still just sat there looking at the dark house I was afraid to go up to.

THESE were giant rubber rollers like the ones on the printing press you see in the window at the newspaper office downtown except they were a zillion times life size, I was running over them and they were rolling fast under my feet, at every step they would break my legs if I just once slipped, the noise was worse than any thunderstorm. Then up in the corner was this lady dancing a waltz in a beautiful gown like a wedding dress but blue, she danced and her blue dress tolled like a bell, I could not reach her. Dad was running alongside me trying to explain, fortunately he could not keep up, I had received two good legs. Then I was in this alley behind this shed with Wesley, Wesley said Go ahead, go on in, so I opened the door but it was the privy and Dad was sitting inside with his pants down around his ankles and his half a head. Blood was filling up his lap. Outside a giant black dog's head was barking showing its yellow teeth then I sat up bolt upright and saw I was in my own van but the dog outside the window was real, and his claws clicking against the van and squeaking down the side were too.

I had locked the doors and rolled up the windows that night before, so it was one-hundred degrees in there and I was sweating like a pig. My heart was pounding in my chest and in my ears.

I figured this big black dog must be tall as a man for he could just put his feet up on the sill and look right in leaving a slobery trail along the windows. He would circle the van, snuffling at all the doors. Then he would be gone and when I looked out I'd see him laying with his head on his paws on the sidewalk.

But if I moved he would stand up like he was expecting me to throw the ball for him and he would come up again and look in. I could see him wondering whether he wanted to bark some more, which he always did.

Then his head snapped around and he dropped back off the side of the van. He trotted up the walk to the house with his tail wagging but on the way he looked over his shoulder and grinned at me. Then I saw the screen door open and the dog slink in.

I untangled myself from Grandma's blankets and crawled between the seats up front. The house did not look so bad in the daylight.

I looked at my watch. I'd slept the sleep of the dead.

Well, I said to myself, may as well face the music.

Have to some time.

You have come thousands of miles.

I looked at myself in the rearview mirror and mashed my hair down a little. I tucked in my shirttails. I looked around for more dogs. I stepped out of the van.

This street of stucco houses with little front yards and picket fences bordered on a kind of no-man's-land filled with junk yards and warehouses. At one end was a big frame house which once upon a time rose all alone in the middle of a truck farm.

At the other end a teeny grocery store sat in the shadow cast by the elevated highway—you could hear the buzz of cars on asphalt. A mile or so distant lay the Pacific Ocean.

Sprinklers were twirling on little patches of lawn. It was already a scorcher—the blacktop was sticky underfoot.

The porch was overhung with sumac. Sumac slush crunched underfoot. I could hear cartoons on the TV.

The dog growled out of the gloom behind the screen door and barked once, but his tail was wagging again and it was more like he missed me, not wanted to tear me limb from limb.

The doorbell button had a little crescent moon on it. I pushed it and it chimed. The dog stood up and pressed his wet black nose against the screen.

"Hi boy," I whispered.

His tail smacked the inside door where it stood ajar.

"You're some watchdoggie, huh?"

Slap-slap. The dog was panting and shifting from one foot to the other. I think if he could have he would have lifted the latch and let me in himself. Instead, he turned around in a circle a couple times, then he vanished. When he came back Uncle Wayne was with him.

FOR "Did you know," my Aunt Mona had said the day we buried Grandma, "there is someone else in California?"

"You'll have to see for yourself," Aunt Mona had said in answer to all my questions.

Aunt Mona told me she had wanted Uncle Wayne to come

to Grandma's funeral but the others wouldn't permit her to invite him. She said they didn't even want to notify him but she had felt it was her duty.

"Why didn't he come then? Why couldn't he come to Grandpa's?"

Aunt Mona said she couldn't answer these questions. I must see him myself if I wanted to know. What she could tell me was that Uncle Wayne asked after Skeezix all the time.

So Uncle Wayne was now living in Southern California and he spent every Thanksgiving with Aunt Mona and Uncle Arthur. They themselves had visited him at his home down the coast. And no one in my family knew this, of course, for as Betty explained to me in whispers once When Uncle Wayne had to go away for his own good it killed Grandpa and we must never utter his name.

"But what does he do for a living? How many kids does he have?"

All Mona would say is "You will see for yourself, he is not the same man."

I knew it was Uncle Wayne right away but he was in some way you could not quite put your finger on whizzen. It was his squinty eyes, but also his face was creased the way paper would be if you balled it up tight and then uncrumpled it and tried to smooth out every single wrinkle.

He looked ready to go somewhere—he was wearing a starched white shirt and dungarees. He just looked at me.

"Hi. Morning. You don't know me, huh?"

"I'm not supposed to order any magazines," Uncle Wayne said in a new voice. "The last time I did that I got in hot water."

"Uh, you don't know me, do you?"

His hand was holding the door like he could close it any second.

"I must look pretty grungy," I said with one of those nervous laughs. "I'm Craig, Uncle Wayne."

Sometimes Uncle Wayne looked like someone who thinks he might have heard the phone ring. This was one of those times.

"Your nephew," I added.

Uncle Wayne just stared.

"I have come all the way from Nebraska."

"I can't sign anything either so come back later," Uncle Wayne said and he closed the door and I heard him lock it.

"Hey!" I said. I knocked on the screen door. I rang the bell.

I stood there trying to take in what I'd seen of Uncle Wayne when his dog's face appeared in the window smiling at me. I stepped off the porch into the flower bed and peered in.

"At least *you're* glad to see me, huh boy?"

"Wuff."

I could see the living room with its suite of furniture, a corner of the hall and a bit of the kitchen. There were magazines on the end-tables and dog-toys on the carpet. Uncle Wayne had corduroy throw-pillows on the couch and cactus plants in wire holders on the walls. Wherever Uncle Wayne had gone to, the cartoons were still on the TV in color.

"Hey, boy, where you going?"

For a while I looked at that empty room like it was a picture, trying to decide what I should do. Should I attempt to reach Uncle Wayne on the telephone? Maybe I should do as he said and come back later. But I was not ready to give up.

So I went around the side of the house and came to a stockade fence with a gate in it. I tried the gate but it was locked. I leaned forward and peeked between the boards and there was Uncle Wayne.

First you could only see his bare back, then that he was in

111

his swim suit now and was sitting in a kid's wading pool out on the lawn, just sitting there in about four inches of water. Maybe he was trying to cool off.

"Uncle Wayne?"

His spine went stiff like I'd shot him.

"Uncle Wayne, please, I came all the way from Nebraska to see you. Don't you remember your own nephew? Don't you remember, you lived with us, Uncle Wayne? Don't you remember your nieces and all your friends? There was Butchy and Martin and they all called you Spike. That was your nickname. And you called me Skeezix, remember? Remember, Uncle Wayne? From Gasoline Alley? I am your only nephew Skeezix."

U NCLE Wayne was so happy to see me when he knew who I was. He kept looking at me and shaking his head. He took me into the house and scrambled up a mess of eggs. He toasted half a loaf of bread. He sat across the kitchen table and watched me eat breakfast like it was the most remarkable thing he ever saw. His dog Ned got so hysterical we had to put him out in the yard then we had to let him in again because he couldn't stop barking.

"I keep asking if you are coming but I never knew you was! Is that your van? What kind of van is that?"

"That's a Chrysler product."

"Is that a good kind? I bet that's a good kind to have."

"It sure ran like a dream coming out here."

"Can I go for a ride in it?"

Uncle Wayne sat there with his elbows on the table and his mouth hanging open and watched me gobble down breakfast.

"I never knew you was coming!" he exclaimed again two minutes later. Ned put his chin on the table and Uncle Wayne pushed it off. "I keep saying Tell Skeezix hello for me and ask him when he is coming to see me, but I never knew you was!"

Uncle Wayne hopped up and down refilling my coffee cup while I gave him all the news.

". . . So then after Harold ran off, Dolores and little Dee moved in with Mama and Mr. Burrows but she is now married again. Betty is married too, to Ron. He works at the radio station. You might have heard they have two kids."

Uncle Wayne just kept politely nodding his head.

"Ron and Betty seem real happy," I said, leaving out the fact that I had never been invited to their home. "And of course Aunt Eileen and Sparky are as ever"—here I felt on shaky ground. "But I sure am rattling on, aren't I?"

I was realizing, Uncle Wayne laughed whenever I laughed.

"Uncle Wayne, I haven't asked you anything about yourself. This is sure a great house," I said, looking around the kitchen with its Formica counter tops and appliances.

"I bet that van'll go ninety," Uncle Wayne said.

"Well, I never took her up to that."

"I bet it will."

"You remember that candy-apple-red Chevy you had, Uncle Wayne?"

Uncle Wayne looked briefly blank, then he said: "I bet she'll carry a ton of stuff."

Oh, boy, I thought, are you stupid. Uncle Wayne doesn't want to talk about the past. It is probably too painful.

Uncle Wayne took my dishes to the sink where he began to wash them. The only sound for a while was the hot water running. He had not mentioned Grandma once. He had not mentioned Grandpa.

Uncle Wayne was sure putting a lot of elbowgrease into it.

113

He was scrubbing with a vengeance. The muscles in his arms and back were rippling. He would hold a dish up and look at it then wash it again. He would rinse it under scalding hot water front and back before he set it in the drainer. I hoped he wasn't mad at me.

I got up and stood at the screen door and looked out at the back yard. Uncle Wayne had two bikes, one a ten-speed, leaning against the patio posts. A baseball bat was laying on the concrete beside his wet prints from the wading pool. Ned slipped his nose under my hand to be petted.

I had not for a second over those few weeks questioned my decision to visit Uncle Wayne, but now that I was here I thought maybe this was not such a good idea after all.

I heard the last of the water belch down the drain. Uncle Wayne was standing at the sink wiping his hands on a towel.

He asked, "Wanna see my train?"

ONCE in my childhood our family went to Sioux City to visit Uncle Walter. Naturally, as soon as we drove off our block, Dolores said she had to pee, and we no sooner passed the back side of the WELCOME TO LINCOLN sign than Betty had to stick her head out the window and upchuck all over the side of our car. After that, as on all our trips, Mama spent most of her time yelling things like Don't pinch her then! and If you don't stop that your dad is going to have an accident and we'll all be killed! But threats and warnings were not the only weapons in Mama's arsenal. She also knew you trapped more flys with honey. Sometimes it was Dairy Queen. On this trip it was Tiny Town.

For on our way to Uncle Walter's happened to be a magical kingdom called Tiny Town and we could get to go if we just let Mama and Dad enjoy their coffee out of the thermos in peace. "It's a whole tiny town with houses and a church and stores," Mama informed us. "There's lights that shine in every window at night and a City Hall with a clock in it and a bell that rings in the church."

"Who rings that bell, Mama?"

"Please do not yell, Betty. You're going to break all our eardrums. I don't know. It just rings."

Then we all screamed When When When Will we get to hear it A tiny man must ring that bell When does it ring Mama Does it just tinkle Did you ever see him Is he the preacher?

"If you are very good all the way," Mama said. So we would be for a while, but soon she would have to say "I don't know if we'll have time to stop by Tiny Town, Larry, what do you think?"

And Dad would say, "I don't know, Janice, depends on if I have to stop this car and spank some child."

We would be quiet then.

It was probably Mama's plan to see Tiny Town all along, because later that afternoon when she said she thought it was somewhere around here, Dad said there probably wasn't anything left of it anymore since the old man died, but Mama asked what made him think that?

"There it is," Mama said, excited, pointing her finger at the sign with its arrow, and Dad swerved off the road and parked the car on the shoulder under some trees.

Us kids jumped out. "You be careful now," Mama said, shutting the car door and putting her purse on her arm. "Aren't you coming, Larry?" she asked Dad through the window, but Dad must have preferred staying in the car.

"Oh, this is such a shame," said Mama as we picked our way along the overgrown path through Tiny Town. "There used to be little stores all along here. This here was an old-fashioned ice cream parlor."

"But there are still lots of houses left, Mama, see?" Betty would not give up. The houses were only wood boxes and all the doors and shutters had only been painted on once upon a time. Vandals had got to Tiny Town. To me there was just enough of Tiny Town left to make you feel much worse than you'd feel good if it had turned out to be as magical as Mama had led us to expect. But to Betty it was like in Peter Pan where you believe hard enough and save Tinkerbell.

"It used to be so pretty," Mama sighed, standing in the middle of town where the shrubs that once served as trees around the tiny bandstand had run rampant. "It was quite a tourist attraction. There used to be lots of cars parked up there on the highway all the time."

"All the windows is broken, aren't they, Mama?"

"I have to go, Mama."

"Oh, and there was a Pullman car diner right down there by the river and cotton candy. Don't pull on me, Dolores. Can't you hold it?"

I never thought of Tiny Town again until I saw Uncle Wayne's train.

It was in the basement family room of his house. This room was finished in knotty pine paneling and also had a knotty pine bar with stools and indirect lighting. There was a wagon-wheel couch and easy chair down there. In one corner was the furnace. But you didn't see any of this at first because Uncle Wayne's train took up almost the whole basement.

Uncle Wayne's train table was plywood set on trestles and it was so big you had to crawl under and come up in the middle if you wanted to reach everything. This table had miles and miles of H.O. track on it, enough for half a dozen trains to run along switchbacks and "S" curves or chug up steep inclines, barrel down straightaways and trace lazy figure-eights without once crashing into each other.

But the chief wonder of this train table was its landscaping.

116

It had not only mountains with tunnels cut through them but rivers with bridges. It had not only a railway station but a town with a general store with a horse-tank and a hitching post. It didn't just have painted rocks and foam rubber trees—it had pines and aspen, mica snow on the mountains, deer and elk, water out of mirror with ducks swimming on it. It had cars on the sawdust roads, a farm with a silo and cows and chickens, sidewalks in the town, picket fences and street lights. There was a wood chopper in the forest, a housewife hanging out the wash, a sheriff in front of the jail, children at play in the one-room-school yard, the farmer in his field, the mailman on his rounds, the stationmaster with his lantern waving on the train.

Uncle Wayne and I must have played with this train for two hours, he showing me everything you could do—the real smoke that came out of the stack, the roundhouse at the foot of the hill, the working water tower. Uncle Wayne demonstrated all the switches, buttons and dials. He turned out the overhead light and made it night. He side-tracked the steam engine and the Limited went streaking through. He delivered milk from the farm and ore from the mines. He rescued stray sheep. We were so into this train, I didn't hear the front door open, nor foot-steps on the floorboards above, nor on the basement steps. But Uncle Wayne must have heard all these, for without even glancing up from the controls, he said "Vernon, look who's here."

UP top Vernon starts the engines and the rear exhausts fart onto the water. The boat slips a few inches away from the dock, then is tugged back by the ropes.

Wayne jumps in and wipes his feet on the mat. He sets down the cooler, stows the mop, then removes the little step ladder and places it on the dock. He unplugs the electric, lashes the cord to the dock. Then he unties the ropes on each side of the boat. Both times, when he bends down, his dark glasses slip off his nose, but they are fastened to a cord around his neck.

Vernon revs up the engine and the boat is free. He steers us out into the traffic. The Rebel flag on the antenna flaps in the breeze, but there is no breeze on the boat yet. We chug through still waters past posts with fish fins nailed to them. The air in this harbor smells like garbage and burnt bird feathers.

I am sitting on one of the chairs that is like a barber's chair with a place between your legs for the fishing pole. Pulleys are clicking and swaying above my head. Wayne runs around being second mate.

When we get beyond the jetty, the sea is no longer calm—it slaps at the Adios. Up top Vernon plies the wheel. The boat rocks back and forth. I am now perched on the gunwale with my feet out in front of me, holding onto the rail, and my stomach is flip-flopping. I watch Wayne polishing up the chrome in the cabin and the marlin figurine that is screwed down like a hood ornament to the ledge in there.

We make our way along the coast past boats big and small, some with sails, some just little motors. Then when we have cruised far out onto the ocean and are mostly alone, Vernon comes down and casts in his lines.

"Wanna try your luck?" he asks.

I say I don't know how.

"Maybe you would like to learn then," says Vernon.

I tell him some other time.

"Suit yourself," he says.

In all that morning, Vernon catches two fish. He kills them and puts them in a plastic bag. Then the sun is high and it is time for lunch.

I don't know if I should eat but I am hungry, so I eat half a hero and drink a beer.

Wayne eats like he is starved and talks nonstop with his mouth full.

When he is finished with his sandwiches, Vernon sits back in the barber's chair and belches. Vernon is dark brown—he is part Mexican and out here almost every day. His hairy arms are covered with naval tattoos and you can see, at the collar of his shirt, his chest must be too. His head is shaved where there was any hair left, so he wears a straw hat. Behind his shades he could be anywhere though often he is, I can feel, staring at me. Wayne is sitting up top now gazing out to sea with a pair of binoculars or picking sunburn off the tops of his feet.

We take off again and chug up the coast. We now pass lots of fishing boats with families in them with dads taking snaps and kids in lifejackets waving little poles out over the choppy waters—these are the type of people Vernon takes out mainly on the weekends.

I have to lay down then. Laying in the cabin I see Wayne fishing now. He is using lots of body language and talking out loud, trying to talk the fish into biting.

Then I have to go down to the little bathroom where I throw up the hero and even, I can tell from the color, some chile from the night before. The barf burns coming up my throat. Barf comes out my nose.

When I flop down on the couch again Wayne sticks his head in upside down.

"You got sick, huh Skeezix? I guess I'm lucky because I never. What? Vernon says I better let you alone."

I did not sleep much last night out on the couch. First of all I drank a lot of beer after dinner and then I was too frazzled to sleep. I was also kept up by Vernon snoring away in his bedroom and everything else Wayne did all day.

On this boat it is frying. I just want to sleep but the sun is knifing in through the cabin window and into my eyes. In scraps on the breeze I can hear Wayne talking to Vernon, then from under my arm I see him sneak down the ladder. He picks up his pole, reels in, baits the hook anew from a bucket, casts out again, sets the pole and sneaks back up the ladder to the plastic booth where the spray cannot reach.

H OW you now, Skeezix?"

I am in the back seat holding my belly.

"You better yet?"

"Stop pestering the boy, Wayne."

Wayne turns around in his seat. His hand thumps a bongo beat on the side of the car. We speed under arches and in between high banks covered with yellow grass. The red sun reaches out and touches all.

"There's that old zoo," comments Wayne up front like he sees it every day when already he has been hinting at the zoo and the mall and that ride in my van.

"How's your leg, Skeezix?"

He keeps asking.

When we get home Vernon suggests Why don't you lay down in Wayne's room before dinner? so I go in there and close my eyes and try not to barf again. My insides don't know they're off the boat and my head is splitting in two. I'm just about to drift off when I hear a rustling in the room and through my eyelashes I see Wayne tip-toe out. But I am able at last to sleep.

I wake up. It is almost dark and I think I must have missed dinner. I check myself out. I feel better.

I can hear the TV and every once in a while Wayne asking a question which Vernon will answer.

120

I lay quiet staring up at the ceiling, every inch of which is covered with Wayne's models. He has jet fighters and bombers and World War II prop planes like the B-52. He has the U-2 spy plane Francis Gary Powers got shot down in over the U.S.S.R. He has not just DC-8s and 727s you write away to the airline for but all the classics: the Lockheed L-649A Constellation, the Sikorsky 2-40, the Curtiss AT-32 Condor, the Ford Tri-Motor 5-AT-C, the Fokker F-VIIA. He has Cessnas. He has vintage bi-planes both German and Allied and too many more to mention. All these hang from the ceiling off thumb-tacks on fishing line and now and again they stir ever so slightly in the breeze coming through the window.

Wayne's bedroom has Space Man wallpaper and a frosted-glass ceiling fixture with rockets on it. His sheets and pillow-cases have Planets on them. All the furniture in his room is painted his favorite color, red.

There is a chest of drawers for his T-shirts, socks, and under-wear. There is his bookshelf full of National Geographics and picture books on Dinosaurs or Cells. There is a drop-front desk with a lion's face on it and lots of compartments inside. There is a captain's chair with a padded seat for reading and a straight-back chair with a spindle back at his model-making table which usually has a plane half finished on it, tubes of glue, camel's hair brushes standing up in a drinking glass and tiny bottles of paint in a rainbow of colors plus gold and silver and military dulls, thinner, bits of sandpaper worn out along the edges, Q-tips and rag twists. No one but Wayne, not even Vernon, is allowed to touch anything on this table.

Wayne has showed me his clothes closet with his suit for church on Sunday and his ties on a rack. He has showed me his shirts and pants on hangers and his many hats arrayed on the shelf. He has showed me his shoes arranged on a metal tree: dress-up oxfords, loafers, sneakers (high-top and low), cowboy boots, hiking shoes, baseball shoes with cleats. Wayne even has ice-skates for the indoor rink. He has also showed me fleece-

lined slippers, moccasins and socks with leather soles he re-
quested for his birthday once.

He keeps all his sports equipment in a closet in the hall.
Wayne owns two more bats and not just a regular glove, which
he has broke in following the instructions on the box, but a
catcher's mitt, mask and protective padding. This he is serious
about because he plays that position on a local team. He has a
beautiful regulation type football. He has the shoulder-pads and
helmet for football too but he does not play anymore because
he got hurt once. He has springs to build up his pectorals. He
has a BB gun Vernon lets him fire at a target on the back of the
garage as long as he is with him. He has a Frisbee Ned has
somewhat chewed up. He has two basketballs, one a brown one,
the other red-white-and-blue. He has a wood-frame tennis
racket and brand new can of balls—these he has not got around
to trying out. Finally, aside from lots of grass-stained, beat-up
baseballs he keeps in this closet, Wayne also has in his room a
baseball signed by all the San Diego Padres which he says he
plans on never playing with.

Somewhere along the line, I guess, Wayne decided he must
be a boy.

WHEN I do get off the bed I am a little light-headed. I go
out into the hall.

The living room is lighted only by the TV. I see the purple
then green walls, then the evening paper scattered all over the
floor, then Vernon on the couch with his stockinged feet up on
the coffee table next to their two empty ice cream bowls nested
together with the spoons resting in them, then Wayne cuddled
up next to Vernon in the crook of his arm. They are watching

situation comedy. They didn't hear me get up. Only Ned hears me now and lifts his head but I imagine he goes back to his nap right after I slip out the front door.

I stand holding onto the door handle of my van. If I leave right now, this minute, tonight, I will leave behind me a dirty T-shirt, a pair of pants, a Mobil map of the U.S., some sticks of chewing gum and Mr. Burrow's electric razor, one he gave me when he replaced it with an up-to-date model.

"Shut the door, don't let Ned come in."

"Wayne, why are we in here if you're not supposed to be in here?"

"Ned'll jump up on the bed and mess it up."

"You said Vernon didn't want you in here."

"That's all right. I can. I can come in sometimes. I just wanna show you."

Vernon's bedroom was neat as a pin. Twin night tables on each side of the bed, twin lamps atop them. Bureau with comb and brush, mirror above, a box for tie-bars and cufflinks. Crucifix where he could see it before he goes to sleep. Venetian blinds half drawn over the windows.

"It's in here."

On the floor of the closet along with shoes and stray dust balls, shoe-shine kit, lost belt with an initial buckle and solitary wire hanger, an Xmas gift box, beat up, back in the corner. Squatting down Wayne brought forth the box, set it on bare floorboards.

"Cross your heart," he whispered.

"I'm sure if Vernon."

"It's all right. Honest." Wayne's eager hands rested on the lid of the box. "Cross your heart."

I do so.

"Promise you won't tell." His face, tilted up at me, begged me to swear, but he did not wait for an answer.

Wayne slid off the lid and one by one began to lift out the magazines, careful to maintain the order of them. When I saw what they were, I said I thought we should put them back now.

"No, no, just a minute. I wanna show you."

"These are Vernon's and I don't think."

"No, I wanna show you. Geez, look at this one. That's a giant one, isn't it, Skeezix?"

I had never seen magazines like this, all men and boys in various full-color poses.

"Can you get yours hard like that yet, Skeezix? I can."

I took the magazine away from Wayne and put it back in the box and then laid the others back in on top of it and closed the box and put it back into the corner on the floor where it belonged.

I let the door handle go. I turn and look up the street and soon I am walking. I walk up the street and I think I probably stop on the corner for a minute under the street light but soon I am running.

DID you know I can run? Did you know I can run, if only like some poor cartoon creature with his tail on fire?

I run under that elevated highway and on the gravel at the side of that old county road curving to the ocean where there is no room to run and cars come whizzing at me honking but I am totally concentrated on the fine mechanics of my running.

I hear my panting but I cannot stop running. Bugs hit my face, a swarm of bugs, I might even swallow some. Pain drills up into my hip, that weed of pain. I remember you.

Why am I running? Why, because I forgot. The bread wasn't

on the table because I forgot the bread and now dinner is almost ready you will have to go back young man, when will you learn to think, he's just plain stupid isn't he Mama, now you get up off that floor and run right back and don't pocket any change you hear, stupidhead stupidhead, you hurry, you'll be lucky if there's any supper left for you young man, now scat!

I was always running. I ran from the bogeyman, I ran from the ghosts on the school swings, I ran from the mailbox on the corner for inside were monsters with their claws waiting to catch children out after nightfall. Oh, I would run. I ran from the ice-thing under my bed lurking to rise up and hang over me when I went to sleep, I must not, and from faces so horrible that flickered in front of my shut eyelids like the tail end of fireworks.

Now I am running in a lurch that is just plain laughable had I breath enough to laugh. It does not even pass for running yet I run and run past loading docks and luncheonettes and trucks' dead headlight eyes behind chain link fence crowned with barb wire until that pain is so red hot like the devil's pitchfork and I have to stop and when I do before my eyes is a sign TOPLESS.

Y OU may think it's a little dead in here, that's cause the girls don't go on till nine. Hi, I'm Candy, what's that you're drinking?"

"Beer," I say.

"I can see that, I mean which kind? They have three kinds of draft here you know. I like the Bud draft best myself. Norma may I have a Bud draft? You want another? And a Bud draft for the gentleman too. You sure worked up a thirst somewhere, didn't you? You work over at U.P.S.? I thought you might cause they get off around this time. Where you work?"

"I don't, I mean I'm not from around here."

"Uh-huh."

"I'm on vacation," I tell her.

"Oh thank you Norma. May I have a coaster too please. That's interesting, from where?"

"Nebraska."

"Oh like Johnny Carson. That's interesting, so you decided to come west for your vacation. I'm from Utah myself but I was a baby. Thank you Norma." Candy whispers, "I am afraid there's no love lost between Norma and me."

She has been leaning toward me with elbows on the bar but now she sits back on her stool and looks at me with squinty eyes.

"Don't get all embarrassed, I'm just looking. Do you know you look a lot like my brother Gary? Gary has all that pretty silky hair too only he wears his longer. Only I think, uh-huh, you're probably even handsomer than Gary. God, now I went and embarrassed myself." She briefly hides her face in her hands then takes another sip of her Bud. "How old are you, about twenty? You mind my asking?"

"Twenty-five."

"Uh-huh, you don't look it, you look mature but not twenty-five. I hope you don't mind my saying that. Gary's just twenty-one."

I give the high sign to Norma. I order a boilermaker for myself and and another draft for Candy.

"That'll sure light your fire," Candy comments. Then she sings:

> Come on baby, light my fire
> Try to set the night on fire

Norma places the beers and the shot glass before us. "This is a nice place," I comment.

126

Candy makes a face. "God, that burns my throat just watching. It's all right but I like the Galahad better, you been there?"

"No."

"It's real nice. You just here or visiting?"

"Visiting."

"Oh, who?"

"Relations."

"Uh-huh. Her name's Lorraine in case you're wondering."

"Oh."

"You can put your tongue back in now."

I hold Candy's pink foot in my hand.

"Course I don't go around looking at the bottom of my feet all the time—see it?"

I allow as how I think I do, a rosy red dot.

"That's from when I stepped on a nail."

I kiss that.

"And this here," she says, pointing at a white line.

I let go her foot and scoot up on the bed.

"That's from a church picnic when we were playing Statues and I kneeled on a broken bottle. That bled like crazy."

I kiss it.

"This is the last one, promise," she says showing me on her arm near the wrist. "So you see you are far from the only one you know."

I can't make it out and lift her arm up to the lamp. She puts her finger on the spot.

"This is the funniest one," says Candy looking at it, "but also the scariest because I could of got cancer and died on the spot. It was this mole I cut off with a pen-knife one day and the school nurse just about passed out. It bled like crazy. I guess that's about it."

I have looked at her forehead and scalp where there are fine lines from when she went through a car windshield on her prom night, and her left thumb where there is a scar from a glass breaking when she was washing it, and her appendix.

There is no scar visible on her arm but I kiss it anyway and then I put my arms around her and kiss her and hold her until she pulls away.

"Just what do you think you are starting now?" she asks. When I take her hand and try to kiss her again she says "I have to change the record" and gets off the bed.

Candy crosses the room and turns over the record, then she goes into the bathroom.

Candy is in there a long time.

There are more joints in a little wood and mother-of-pearl box next to the bed but I feel I should ask first.

"Aren't you dressed?" she asks when she comes out. She has put her clothes back on and made up her face.

"Why?"

"What do you mean?" she asks.

"You wanna go somewhere?" I ask like a dumb-bell.

Candy throws my jeans at me.

"This has been nice but I have to go back, so I would appreciate my money," she says.

I sit on the edge of the bed. I hold my jeans in my hands. I ask What money.

"My money."

"I don't get it."

"My money!" Candy yells somewhere between mad and hurt.

"You didn't say anything about money," I am able to get out.

"I said sawbuck!"

"You said I will need a sawbuck."

"Yes, I said I will need a sawbuck!"

"I thought you meant, you know."

Candy stands in the middle of the floor with one hand on her hip, her purse dangling from the other.

"No. I don't know what you mean. You know, what!"

"Protection," I croak.

All the air goes out of Candy. She plunks herself down on the foot of the bed. She mutters something.

"Pardon?" I ask.

"I said asshole hick. Why do you think I had you up here?"

"I thought you liked me."

Candy starts crying but when I try to comfort her she punches me in the stomach. Then she gets up and gets some Kleenex and blows her nose.

"I'm sorry, honest."

"Dumb asshole hick, what do you think this is?"

"I didn't know."

Candy blows again. "Well I'm not supposed to say this but I lied," she says turning on me with a sneer. "I have never had to work so hard in my life!"

"I know. I could tell."

"Tell what?"

"I wasn't any good. Here. Here's my billfold. Here. I lied too. I never did it before."

"I knew that." Candy sniffs.

"But I do love you. That's the truth."

"God, how much you got in here? God, you are a hick, aren't you?"

It is one a.m. by the time Candy drops me off and the house is dark. Ned is waiting inside the front door.

"Good boy, good Neddie, shhh."

Vernon is snoring away in his bedroom.

"Shhh, boy, shhh."

I peek in on Wayne in his bed. In the darkness his room with all the model planes hanging from the ceiling is like a cave with bats sleeping hanging upside down.

129

THE next morning I am waiting for Vernon to say something but he doesn't, just eyes me over the rim of his coffee cup.

"Hi, Skeezix, morning, Skeezix," Wayne says with his mouth full of cornflakes. "I guess today's the day, ain't it?"

"What day?"

"The zoo, Skeezix, and maybe the mall. Don't you remember? You promised today."

"Oh, yeah."

"Don't you forget to feed Ned," Vernon tells Wayne but he is looking at me.

So before he goes to work Vernon draws me a map even though Wayne keeps saying I know the way, I know the way.

Wayne keeps running ahead. First we visit the sea lions but we are no sooner there than he wants to see the African beasts. Everywhere we go he reads the signs out loud and asks me what I think. The few people patronizing the zoo today think Oh how sad, that man is retarded. It was the same way at the gas station where I got directions to the house that first night—Oh you mean Gonzalez, the one with the slow cousin. And at the grocery store, everyone pitying him—Why, Wayne is our star kecher, ain't you? said the man behind the counter.

Wayne loves this zoo so much, he calls the animals by their Christian names.

After the apes and their antics it is time to eat so we stop at the snack bar and I buy us hot dogs. We sit at a picnic table under the trees.

"Did you know this is the biggest zoo anywhere? We have a bigger zoo than anyone." Wayne reads all sorts of zoo facts to me from a flyer then he takes out his billfold and counts his money. "Exactly ten dollars and twenty-five cents. That F-111 is only seven ninety-eight plus tax so I will have almost two dollars left over."

"Turn here, turn here, this is the way!" Wayne yells, so I do but we get lost and have to stop and consult Vernon's directions. "Oh, yeah, this is right," Wayne says as the mall swings into view. "I could of sworn that was the street. You know something Skeezix? I think maybe that was the old street that they changed just the other week."

When we park in the lot Wayne is careful when he gets out to see the door is locked without my having to remind him. So I say to myself This is going okay.

But in K-Mart after we pick out a toothbrush for me and buy Wayne's F-111, we are walking out through a set of double doors the other side from the way we came in, but the outside doors won't open. Wayne is pushing at the doors and I then see the EXIT FRONT OF STORE sign and I am about to say so when a store guard not even carrying a weapon opens the inside door and he is going to say something too and Wayne freaks out.

"I'm sorry, I'm sorry!" Wayne says, backing into the corner. "I just wanted to tell you."

Wayne squeezes along the wall and past the guard out the other door and then he is walking fast backwards down the aisle in the store away from us tripping over his own feet saying he's sorry, he's sorry. The guard is saying What is he, some kind of nut? I'm yelling Wayne it's all right he just wanted to tell us.

AS soon as Vernon mailed the letter he wanted it back.

He imagined, though, if you went up to one of the windows and asked for your letter, what the man behind the grill would say.

"Look here, bud," he would say. "What I have been trying to tell you is that as soon as you drop that letter in that slot over there it is in the hands of the U.S. Post Office. What I am trying to tell you is that it don't belong to you any more."

"Well it sure as hell don't belong to the Post Office."

"What I have been trying to tell you is that it belongs to the party you yourself designate as addressee. Now maybe you'll let me serve some of these good people waiting behind you?"

He returned to his rented room and attempted to read a paperback but the letter tormented him. He had stated one thing correctly in it: he was poison all right. The rest of what he wrote he stopped believing the very second the letter slipped out of his fingers into the mail.

He paced his room and cursed this day that was supposed to be his deliverance. He had sat up much of the night composing the letter—try after try lay in the wastebasket. Now he wanted to sob when he remembered that he'd even pondered not signing it because, what if eyes other than those intended read it?

He cursed and cursed himself. By some stretch of the imagination, he might have been forgiven when he met Wayne for not

132

resisting once. But, no, he had succumbed again and again and took them both down in flames.

Then in Honolulu he had a chance to redeem himself but he did not let the kid go. Instead he immediately made all sorts of promises he knew he could not keep even as he was making them. Fortified by whiskey, he told all sorts of lies, and then when he saw he was losing, took a different tack and played Devil's advocate, pretending to argue the pros and cons. He knew not to try and kiss Wayne. Instead he went on to recall sadly those few times they had managed to spend together. He concluded by saying it must not be allowed to happen again for both their sakes, he just felt lucky to be able to say good-by like this after all that had happened. Then in the silence following, Vernon's hand sought Wayne's on the bedspread and found it.

He did not have the courage to kill himself. How many times had he stood at the sink with the razor blade hanging fire over his wrist and then backed out? How many times had he imagined behind his closed eyelids the window sash rise, his feet on the sill, the sidewalk? But he was too yellow.

He stood in the middle of the floor choked up with love.

So Wayne didn't answer the letter and that comforted him somewhat because he felt that if he was determined to do evil at least he had managed to set in motion events beyond his control for the better. He even felt a little proud of his handiwork, reasoning that he if he himself had received such a letter, he wouldn't reply in a million years.

The months wore on. He still could not land a job worth shit. Then one day almost by chance he was tipped off by what must have been a fellow traveler as to why. He rushed home in a state of excitement. He felt almost joyful when he sat down and wrote Wayne what he had found out—that everyone knows there's a code on the confirmation form. Though the words "one of our own kind told me" seemed about to flow out of the tip of the pen he held in his hand, he checked them, still fearful even now of reprisals and blackmail. As it was, he knew and did not know. He was too terrified to know more than he did.

But with a trembling hand he continued his letter and did not pause again until he reached the end, where he wondered how he should sign himself—deciding at length on his name alone, hoping the fact of the letter itself would some day plead his in his favor.

When this letter came back marked NO LONGER AT THIS ADDRESS RETURN TO SENDER, Vernon reflected that he'd got what he wanted and deserved after all.

So after all his arrogant boasts to family and friends, Vernon ended up going back to what he knew best before he ever set foot in the Navy to better himself and rise above his circumstances. Throughout his teenage years he had worked on excursion vessels. Now, used to command but unfit for it, he worked on other people's boats until he had enough saved for one of his own.

So Vernon prospered. He bought his house but did not furnish it. Who for? He thought of Wayne less and less to be sure—sometimes he thought it was like his heart was in the deepfreeze freezing inch by inch and there was just a minute lukewarm spot left in the center of it, and most times he was glad of that. But he never forgot and would not have entirely even if this had been the end of Wayne. Of course it was not, because one day Vernon came home from work to find this forwarded by his family in Chula Vista:

January 5, 1961

Dear Chief:

I bet you never thought you'd hear from the likes of me again. Here I am though writing to say hello.

As you must know I was put in the hospital against my will but it worked out O.K. They let me out a few days ago as you can see from the above it was, as they say, a new year's present. So I am out.

Thanks for your many kindnesses candy postcards and so on.

I have little to report. I'm a little disoriginated as is to be expected. I'm getting used to Kearney and this hotel. The food isn't so good but there's lots of it after you've been where I have. I was give a job.

Well that's about it. I hope you will forgive this.

Hi from Wayne.

Vernon sat in his chair whilst dusk turned to dark. He cried, read this letter, and cried again. He jumped up at one point and ran to the phone but he had second thoughts.

He was supposed to be so smart, but he never knew until this letter: those events he had been pleased to think were out of his control, weren't those the very ones he'd had the most say in all along? The man who made Wayne meet him in the paint locker that first night surely could have made him come to California garage or no garage. The man who said "You don't know it yet but you love me" surely should have known it was himself in love he meant. The man who could write such a letter throwing Wayne over surely could have talked it into thin air; after all, he was the one who wrote it.

He sat in his chair holding onto the arms and figured out what he had wrought.

135

Of course the punishment never fits the crime, but he thought he knew pretty well what had been done to Wayne in the hospital, and he thought how peculiar that it was exactly what he had asked for himself and been denied by three doctors, but Wayne got it gratis when he didn't want it.

It was rich. Instead of writing to place the blame, Wayne thanked him for kindnesses he never did. He would have done them had he known! But the fact was he had made sure he'd not known and had not done them, and even so, how could kindnesses from him possibly be called kindnesses given who they came from?

He wondered and wondered what he should do now. He began to sweat and shake, sitting in the dark. He was scared Wayne might someday come to find him because if he was Wayne he'd kill him.

Around midnight, he turned on the light and read Wayne's letter again. It was not, he decided, a letter a killer would write, unless maybe Wayne had become vastly cunning as a result of his cure.

He tried to figure out why, beyond the misunderstanding over the gifts, Wayne wrote him in the first place. It was of course not just to say hello. Maybe Wayne had even exposed himself to danger by writing him of all people. Vernon felt then he must protect Wayne somehow—and yet how could he know he was not the one who most needed protecting?

He did not know. And he figured, in the first light of dawn, he could not know. He could sit. He could do that. He was able to do that. That's all he'd been doing in the intervening years while events spun out their webs distant from him. Finally, though, Vernon decided he had already done enough along that line and at least he could try however feebly making amends. Finally he did get up and go to the phone but by that time Wayne had checked out, no forwarding address.

ALMOST a year and two detective agencies later, Vernon found him, on a farm outside Beatrice.

Maybe it was not so odd that Wayne, after voyaging around the world in his youth, seemed disinclined to travel in his native land more than one hundred miles from where he was born. How many of his sailor brothers had turned out the same? Nor did the private detective find it odd. Most people, he told Vernon driving out there, even those you'd think would most want to run the farthest, stick close to home.

The old lady swore on a whole stack of bibles no such person ever set foot on her property but they found him hiding in the barn. He looked like someone out of a war. He'd been worked hard and was dreadfully underweight. His hair was matted down. He was lousy. His clothes and his skin seemed of a piece. The detective pulled an old quilt out of the car trunk and threw it over the back seat. They were finally able to coax him into the car, the old lady calling from the porch all the while how she was going to set the sheriff on them for kidnap. On the ride to Omaha he was stone silent.

"Well we sure as shootin can't take him into no respectable house like this," said the detective, almost jolly, in the car, so once in Omaha they drove right to the Salvation Army to get him shaved and de-loused. While this was being done, Vernon went out and bought him shoes and socks and underwear, chino pants and a chambray shirt.

Vernon sat up that night all night in the motel and watched Wayne sleep. He asked himself, what did Wayne dream? What secret did he know? For it was evident from his answers to their questions that afternoon, something more had happened to Wayne since his release. Now he could not remember his age, he could not remember who his people were, he could not remember growing up or his naval career.

Vernon brought him home and in the days that followed Wayne seemed to come to himself more. He did continue, however, for many months to insist on two things: that his name was Skeezix and he was still in the state of Nebraska.

B Y and by Wayne came into his new self, and never did there seem such a happy creature. And yet many was the night Wayne cried out in his sleep and Vernon rushed to his room, where the glare of the overhead light switched on would reveal him tossing and jerking in his bed with teeth chattering. Other nights Vernon would think he was waking to the sound of God's judgment approaching them on leaden feet only to realize it was again Wayne rocking in his sleep, it was his head against the headboard of his bed, and Vernon would lie helpless and contemplate not going in and trying to stop him, for at these times some part of Wayne took over, terrible and determined, and possessed him all night.

Many was the night Vernon cried his own self to sleep alone in his bed like a widow lady, hands on top of the coverlet, but rosary beads nevertheless unsaid in the top bureau drawer.

Vernon had to be vigilant and not just the way you must be for the sake of someone who is like Wayne but in other ways too. For this could happen any time—Vernon would catch himself looking at Wayne, or worse Wayne at him, his eyes seeming to mean things he could never. At these times which

138

seemed to wax not wane, Vernon knew the devil must take great pains to furnish hell with all sorts of things of rare beauty, beautiful paintings and statuary, gold, silver and jewels, carpets like mosses, ceilings like sunsets, perfect fragrant rose trees, peacocks and perfumed fountains.

Vernon could ask himself what they were until he was blue in the face but no satisfactory answer was ever forthcoming. He was dad, brother, uncle, cousin, bosom buddy, he was protector and confessor, friend, dictator, comforter, he was Midas— everything he could give he gave and everything he had to give was 24 carat pure gold coin of the realm in Wayne's eyes. But nobody knew he was Judas too.

Really they were each other's life sentence. They were now together forever, more wed than man and wife, more tied than mother and child. Yet when they were taken separate, Wayne was at least Peter Pan in that no-man's-land he made up. But Vernon, left without hope or even self-pity—Vernon was now a nothing.

B UT you saved him!" I exclaim when Vernon has finished his tale.

But Vernon looks at me a minute then snorts like I am hopeless. He goes to the ice box to get another beer.

Wayne is finally sleeping in his room after having cried all afternoon and even when he was taking his bath.

"But there must be a doctor who knows how to fix this," I reason. "Maybe the Mayo Brother's clinic or somewhere like that. Maybe there is an expert in this. Maybe there are new medicines for this. I could take him there."

"Shit," says Vernon—the sound is like the air-brakes on a

semi. "You can't even get Wayne to the dentist. He's got a busted crown right now needs repair but you can't even get him in the chair."

"But he is my Uncle Wayne. He is not a boy. I am Skeezix, not him."

"And I am the Shadow," says Vernon with a little smile because these are nicknames Wayne himself gave to us, so if we like it or not we will always be like blood-brother members of his secret club even when we are ninety.

"But don't he ever want to grow up? Don't he miss his family? Does he even know his mama and his dad are dead?"

"They are like people he never met," says Vernon, sitting astride his chair. "Your aunt found that out when she would insist on driving down here after your grandad died. He don't want to remember, see? And why should he," says Vernon, his voice growing angry, "why should he remember after what was done to him, God forgive me. What more you people want done to him?"

I am running.

Dad is back. Dad is back. Dad is back with his knobby pink hands holding my wrist bones and making me walk on his shoes around the room.

De-dum, de-dum, de-dum!

Dad dad dad is pumping my arms up and down and I jerk around like poor Pinocchio.

Then Dad is Washington Irving without his head, he is galloping down the road in the dark to get you, he is behind you, he is headless in his giant

140

and his ten fingers shoot fire like a spaceship, deadly weapons like Dad's gun, his gun he blew off his head with.

NO DAD!

Dad dad dad chops me down in the dust on that road makes me eat a mouthful so I can get used to it.

Then he sits on my back and takes my poor leg and twists and twists it like in wrestling on TV.

Please, please, I just got it!

But he takes out this rusty old toothed saw and saws away and gnaws away and chews off all the loose scraps of skin with his teeth.

Yum, yum, so delicious!

Now this time, this time I must watch Dad in the basement where he is always

all all all alone.

Front-row seat!

He pulls the trigger. Pulls it. There are Dad's brains. Like confetti. They fall in pieces. Soft like snow.

Fall.

All.

Over.

DON'T cry, Skeezix."

It is Wayne next to my couch.

"Don't cry, Skeezix, don't cry."

It is like I ran a hundred miles.

"You had a bad dream, huh?"

I can only lay there and cry but worse than he cried all day because no sound will now come out of me.

"Don't cry."

But I can't stop so Wayne lays down on me and holds me and kisses my eyes and Ned licks my hand and we stay like that.

AT Grandpa's funeral I was on one side of Mama and Mr. Burrows was on the other. Grandma and Uncle Walter sat before us in the front pew. You could only see the top of Grandma's bitty head.

There was a curtain you could watch the congregation through but they couldn't see you. Grandpa's coffin was up there surrounded by flowers.

We are now a family once more is what I thought sitting there—I still thought at that point they would bring me home sometime. Mama held my hand in hers though I felt it should be the other way around for Mr. Burrows had told me to be a man and a comfort.

Tears dripped off Mama's chin as the preacher told of Grandpa's virtues, of his early life and long service to the railroad. Since Grandpa did not have a chance to retire before he died, the preacher said, he fell in the line of duty. He told how this man raised a fine family under trying circumstances.

Every time the preacher said something that hurt, Mama squeezed my hand hard. She reeled in that pew from the blows the preacher was dealing her.

Our Father who art in heaven

I looked out over the congregation. Grandpa was the best. He had so many friends. I had been out with Grandpa on the motorcar and saw how his men loved him. The white hankies rose and fell out there. I loved Grandpa too but he never knew and now it was too late. I wanted to wedge myself into the space at our feet and hide under Grandma.

Then it was over.

We went out into the hall. Mama still had ahold of my hand. I could see through the open door into the chapel, men were gathering around Grandpa's coffin. I knew we were going to bury him now.

Grandpa will never come back.

I started bawling. Mr. Burrows said "They are just going to take him into the vestibule now so the mourners can view him one last time."

I would never see Grandpa again. Saturday he was eating his dinner and then he died when I was downtown seeing the movie without asking if I could. Strangers were getting to say good-bye to Grandpa and I never.

"I wanna see Grandpa!"

Mama's face was red. Her mouth was twisted up. She gave

me a shove down the hall for last night I had said No, no, I don't want to.

"Then go and see him!"

I hesitated. In front of me were the people filing out. Behind me Mama said "Go and see him while you still can." I felt she was telling me not to and if I did she hated me, but she said Go again.

So I turned and walked down that hall. I do want to see Grandpa. I have a right to. I am his grandson.

Almost all the people were gone but the few clustered around the coffin drew back since I was his grandson and one man there held his palm out and open like he was saying Step right up! like the barker at the fair.

I did. I looked in. The coffin's insides were pink satin. Grandpa wore his blue suit. He was like a doll of himself in that pink box. I looked at his face. Grandpa wore make-up so what was missing were the lines and the many broken veins. Grandpa's nose was like a hammer head from death—the bones stuck out and the rest of his face looked like it was leaving now.

I asked myself Is this what Dad looked like?

No, Uncle Bill said Dad blew a hole in his head when he left him alone. Uncle Bill never said where in Dad's head, so it may have been in the mouth. It may have been to one side. Maybe there was no head left, I would speculate, maybe a a great deal.

I studied Grandpa's face. I could tell you anything about it.

All this time I was screaming and bawling then the funeral men came to close the coffin. I stumbled down the hall to the exit. In the driveway a black station wagon stood with the back door open waiting for Grandpa. Across the lawn was a black limousine and Mama beckoning to me from inside. I took out my handkerchief and blew my nose and tried to act fourteen. All the way across that lawn I said to myself "Don't fall, don't fall, not now."

WAYNE lays beside me sleeping in his shorts white against his dark skin in the dark with one leg and one arm cast over me breathing deep, but I myself can only stare into the dark outside the open window with the sumac crowding against the screens and think how here I thought all those years Uncle Wayne killed Grandpa because Betty said so—she said Because he had to be sent away for his own good but now I know: I did it.

> Two little chillun
> Layin in bed
> One of them sick
> De other half dead

This must be what Mona sent me here for to see for myself, so I would know what dreadful calamity all my lies brought about in the lives of so many including Vernon now too. Candy is right, I was not the only one who got chewed up. I would cry if I had any more tears left. I ask myself what kind of child would make up the things I did?

Wayne stirs against me, he is slobbering on my shoulder, he smells like toothpaste. I let my head rest against Wayne's.

Vernon is snoring up a storm down the hall, he sounds like a kitchen full of percolators.

I reach down, I free my dick stirring under the sheet and I wonder had Wayne cum ever since he became a boy? Does he know what it's really for? Did he learn again all by himself the way I did? Did he learn anything he knows from Vernon's secret books? Is he like Ned who when it sticks out red like a raspberry gets a hurt quizzical look on his face? Does Wayne only wake ashamed like he wet the bed?

I rub my dick through the sheet, something I have loved to do since I discovered I had one at Wayne's age and long before Mama discussed that handkerchief with me.

Uncle Walter and his wife and their little girl lived in a bungalow house in Sioux City like a Hansel and Gretel cottage with valentines on the shutters and tires on the lawn whitewashed and planted with sweet peas. When we pulled up in their driveway the three of them came out on the front porch to greet us, Uncle Walter holding his evening paper folded so as not to lose his place, Aunt Ivy in her good apron because dinner was all ready, sitting in the oven, the Jell-O in the icebox waiting for us to arrive, Cousin Lou dolled up in a ruffled frock.

"Here's the travelers," Uncle Walter said.

"Yessir," said Dad.

"Well I guess you better come in."

Lou danced attendance on the grownups. Us kids trudged in behind.

"You keep Lou so nice," Mama commented, taking off her head scarf. "I'm afraid my girls just don't appreciate pretty things."

"I preciate pretty things, Mama."

"Oh, Lou loves to dress up for company, don't you, honey?"

Dad took me upstairs to the bathroom.

"Let's see now," he said, closing the door behind us.

Dad kneeled down. He helped me unbutton the suspenders

146

on my overalls. The metal parts clinked on the tile. I shucked down my shorts.

"Whatcha doing?" he asked.

"Wee-wee."

"Well dang boy, you don't have to sit down to do that do you?"

"I don't know."

"Well no, a big boy like you is big enough to stand there and wee-wee right into the bowl, ain't he?"

"I guess."

"Well why don'tcha then?"

So Dad steered me over to the bowl and stood behind me with his hands on my shoulders and he taught me, he taught me how to pee against the side of the bowl and not into the water so no one can hear you.

T HIS couch is narrow. Wayne lays heavy against me. If I shift I'm afraid he is liable to roll off. I ease my arm up out from between us. Then with my free hand I lift up his sleeping head.

"Hum," Wayne says.

I slip my arm around him and pull him close. His breath beats ragged on my chest then soon regular. I bend down my head and taste his hair. I find my dick again.

And then there was that first time when Wesley and me were spelling words on each other's back then we would have to guess what. In the silence in Wesley's bedroom it was almost like I could hear his fingernail rasp making block letters on my skin, sort of the same way that when you eat snow you think you can taste it though you are probably only tasting your wet mitten.

It was all his idea. He wanted to do it more than I did but I found I liked it, not at first as much as feeling myself. When his started spurting white stuff it scared the daylights out of me, but I learned to like the feel of his hand like mine but not.

Blindly I slide my hand under the sheet. My hand comes into contact with my bare skin.

Wayne's smooth chest sticks sweaty to my side. The fingers on my hand on the arm holding him are starting to tingle but I can still feel his ribs.

I lay there holding my hard dick looking over at the window where the sky is maybe going to appear soon.

That night in my tent the night Wesley wouldn't do it and pretended he was sleeping I remembered what he once told me and secretly I felt between my legs.

Wesley was right, that was the softest part of the human male anatomy.

Under my balls was a little soft pad of flesh, no hair on it yet, and it was easy to picture this was a teeny trap door, and what if inside you had a teeny-weeny baby the size of a plastic Jesus under the tree, just like girls must have inside them before the boy sprinkles it and it grows into a real one, but you could never if you were a boy because this did not open.

I see if I can time my breathing to Wayne's.

Wayne has made sure after he was hurt he will be forever like the Sleeping Beauty, won't he, in that glass coffin or was it Snow White?

Vernon bends over the glass. It is the purest crystal.

This glass coffin is supposed to keep leaves and junk out but you can see where a spider has already started a web up in one corner and there is the thinnest layer of dust on Wayne's pale face. Soon it may be too late for other insects and even snakes may move in and what if they start eating him alive? Creeping vines may in time split in two the marble base of the crystal coffin that is like the beautiful rose bowl Mama once had before I accidentally broke it. It was a clear glass globe. You filled it

148

with water and floated a rose in it then screwed the base on with its rubber ring. Mama would hold that globe over the sink and slowly turn it right-side up so the rose would not drown. I used to watch her. I thought Mama was so wonderful. Vernon raises his fist but even he is too afraid to shatter the glass.

If I do what I'm thinking of doing would Wayne wake like Old Rip Winkle in Washington Irving?

It is funny because I wonder, if I do this and it works and Wayne thus grows up would he turn out bigger than me? I guess this is because my Uncle Wayne was such a hero to me once. I have to remind myself I am a full-grown man, in fact I am now taller than him, maybe I am even stronger too. I noticed Wayne's endurance is good but playing catch the other day I knocked him off balance a couple of times . . .

God what if this makes me one too? I do not think I am one God but what if I am after all? If you are a man and you do it are you one?

Oh, God, what if this works but it turns out they don't love each other anymore?

All the time I am running my trembling fingers along it just barely touching it, skimming the skin's surface.

Wayne's body against the length of mine is sometimes heavy, sometimes I can't feel it at all. If I let myself, I will get scared— because you see for long moments there is no line between us. Wayne's hand on my belly rides like a ship on waves. On the other side of his head Wayne's breath in little gasps falls like air puffs on my breast.

THAT summer when the folks across the bayou from Grandpa and Grandma still had a privy but Grandpa said I was too little, if I tried it out I would fall in. That summer when Grandpa stole cinders from the railroad for his driveway and Dad told us kids they were just borrowed—Grandma said to Mama How they stick to the soles of your shoes and track up the kitchen! That summer when Betty informed me Our Lord was crucified on one of Grandma's clothesline posts but it was a secret which one, the Angel Gabriel had told only her.

That Fourth of July when Grandpa broke the porch swing spraining Grandma's pinky finger in the bargain, when every sparkler lay dead as a doornail bent and tortured underfoot, when Dad pulled the plug out of the icecream maker to drain the salt water which I tasted on my finger as it spurted out then it oozed then drip-dripped over the edge of the porch killing the weeds in the flower bed Grandma mysteriously never had any luck with, when Betty got to lick the paddles but she licked axle-grease too by mistake, when Mama took me in and swabbed vinegar all over my sunburn to cool it, when piggy Dolores took up the whole couch with her head in Mama's lap sucking her thumb and kicked me every time I even moved, when Mama made me go upstairs saying I was cranky because I cried, when I lay on the bed in Uncle Wayne's room at the top of the stairs because he was sailing around the world, listening—to their voices, so soft, it was their own house but they sounded for all the world like people coming in late to the movies saying Excuse me please Thanks Oh so sorry, listening

150

to the firecrackers that sounded like popcorn popping far away in the city park where you sat on waxed paper to go dangerous fast down the slide with two bumps, listening to the thump of passing cars' tires on the rails over the crossing (they recoil and rear up out of control a minute in the air), listening to the Kamikaze moths dive-bombing the window screens dying to get in to die and the racket of the crickets and the whirr down in the bayou where I knew a coffee can yet floated in the stinking water since I could not sink it that afternoon by throwing stones at it.

Tonight petting Dolores's head Mama is like a different one from the one you knew. Dad is quiet, so drunk he is sober again, though you must not forget he could turn on a dime. Grandpa is sitting chawing on a toothpick in his chair. The cancer is taking root in him already. Grandma's crochet needles if you could hear them would be making quick teensy-weensy clicks— the rainbow-colored thread is unspooling patient at her side. Betty is sprawled asleep under the coffee-table. I upstairs am maybe asleep, maybe not. You did not have to be awake to remain within the circle of their voices, their voices were like the ringing in your ears from those cherry-bombs those boys set off on the bridge too close to little children Grandma said.

That night when Dad came up and picked me up off Uncle Wayne's bed when he carried me careful down the stairs (so steep in that house they were more like the ladder to a hayloft than proper stairs, Dad liked to point out) and put me in the back of the car when I still pretended to be fast asleep when Dad tickled me so I had to wake up even if he did not make me giggle when I opened my eyes when I saw I was staring into his full of hurt waiting for him to say something anything though he never did.

THE sky is growing lighter.

I think it is.

The sky gets lighter, Wayne breathes on ignorant, I can see through the leaves now it is cloudless, it is going to be a beautiful day, today they are going to try landing on the moon.

I hated Dad but when he was dead I used to miss him like I never did before. I was so sorry he was dead and all his dreams came to naught. I used to go out on the back porch and look up at the night sky and try to think Dad is watching over me. (Surely God let Dad into heaven!) I used to try to imagine Dad gazing down upon me through some kind of porthole in the clouds watching over me and still trying to love me as I know he did try so in real life.

I would think on those nights, if Dad had me he would not have had to blow off his head with a gun.

But then I would remember how Dad came this close to killing me too.

But this morning I try to feel, looking out that window, Dad is still up there.

But maybe it's because the astronauts are up there now—I can't quite believe anymore. So I try to imagine Dad is all around us. Mama always said she could not be a good Catholic because she did not see any point in worshipping in any church, she used to say God is in all Nature, all around, in the flowers and the birds and the running rills and the blue sky. I used to snicker up my sleeve at this because we all knew Mama hated the great outdoors, but now I try imagining Dad is all around us like Him, in every atom, even in my hair and toenails. Maybe Dad is in my blood.

Like, if Dad is not up there, is he whispering in my ear right now he is still here?

Yes, Dad, yes?

I lay as still as I possibly can. I lay there for the longest time listening. I try listening.

Then I lift Wayne's hand up from off my belly and gently place it down there.